Ana Rocha:

Shadows of

Justice

Ana Rocha: Shadows of Justice

Ammar Habib

Glenda V. Mendoza

ANA ROCHA: SHADOWS OF JUSTICE

Copyright © 2018 by Ammar Habib

Cover Art by Fiona Jayde

Printed in the United States of America

First Edition: February 2018
First Printing: February 2018

ISBN: 978-1985736139

For more information, please visit:
www.ammarahsenhabib.com

Other works by the Ammar Habib include:

THE HEART OF ALEPPO

MEMORIES OF MY FUTURE

DARK GUARDIAN

DARK GUARDIAN: A NEW DAWN

DARK GUARDIAN: LEGENDS

DEDICATION

This book is dedicated to all the officers and first responders who put their lives on the line every day in order to help keep us safe.

Ammar would also like to dedicate this book to:
His mother, father, brother,
And his great-grandfather, Amir Baig Mirza,
A police inspector and the first writer in his family

Glenda would like to specially dedicate this story to:
Her grandmother, Glenda Vivian Rocha,
And to her father, mother, brothers, and daughter

TABLE OF CONTENTS

SETTING & LIST OF CHARACTERS

SETTING:
Houston, Texas in 1999

PROTAGONIST:
Ana Rocha – a 22-year-old Hispanic woman born and raised in Houston

MAIN CHARACTERS:
Bryan Fulton – Ana's partner
Captain Scott "Cap" – Ana's superior officer
Ben Smith – an FBI agent
Queen Bee (Ebony Thorne) – the head of the *Los Familia* gang
Vinny the Rat – Queen Bee's infamous lieutenant

ANA ROCHA'S FAMILY:
Angela – Ana's deceased sister
Ramon – Ana's brother
Laura – Ana's sister-in-law, Ramon's wife

INTRODUCTION

Thank you for picking up a copy of **Ana Rocha: Shadows of Justice!** We certainly hope that you enjoy reading this thrilling adventure as much as we enjoyed creating it!

One of the main original motivations for writing this novel was to show a narrative from a police officer's perspective. We wished to present a story that showcases some sacrifices that not just narcotics officers, but all officers, make. In today's day and age, this side of the coin is often overlooked.

Glenda's background with law enforcement, particularly her former experience as an undercover narcotics officer, allowed us to ground this story in reality and keep it as true as possible to what an officer might face in the field. This definitely shows in our protagonist, Ana, and many of the scenarios she faces.

We'd like to end by thanking you. An author is nothing without his readers, and we truly appreciate your support. We do not take it lightly when readers select this book out of the countless works available. We look forward to the honor of hearing your thoughts someday. Glenda and I hope this story pulls you in and that you enjoy the ride! Thank you.

Your friends,
Ammar & Glenda
February 2018

CHAPTER 1
TRIAL BY FIRE

There are times when I'm sure I see her.

She's standing in the doorway. She's watching me from the hilltop. She's staring back at me from the mirror. But then I remember that these are nothing more than mirages.

Because she's never coming back.

***

The two men rush me, switchblades in hand.

Come on, Ana. Get control of yourself. Remember everything. Don't get emotional. Predict and attack—predict and attack.

Miller is the closer of the two. The right side of his body is cocked back. He'll lead with his right. A quick glance at the lackey tells me that he's waiting for his boss to make the first move. Blood running from his broken nose, the lackey keeps his eyes on Miller. Once his boss attacks, the lackey will follow to finish me off.

Or so he thinks. My heart is racing—my mind runs wild. But I control my breathing like I was taught.

Let him make the first move. He'll come at you with the knife. Ignore the blood and block out the pain. Concentrate on him. Patience... patience... patience.

There is a moment of calm. Then he makes his move.

Miller lunges at me with his knife. But I already saw it coming and sidestep him with ease. The blade runs right by me. As he misses, I step up into him.

Attack with precision. Don't go for the finishing blow. Just stun him to even out the odds. Finish him later.

My open palm strikes Miller right below his diaphragm, knocking the wind out of him.

"Uuuff—"

I bring my knee up. It hits him right between his legs. Before he can even fully register the pain, I powerfully strike his skull with my elbow. He spits out a stream of blood.

But I don't get the chance to look over my good work. Feeling something behind me, I twirl around just in time to dodge the lackey's knife.

The fight's not over yet.

***

A Few Days Earlier:

My first assignment on the new job: buy crack.

It's not what you might be thinking. I'm not a drugee. Neither is the person who ordered me to get the drugs. I'm not a dealer either. In fact, I'm the complete opposite. I'm the type of person that puts dealers behind bars. Or, at least, that's what I've just become.

They did not bother to teach me much my first day as an undercover narcotics officer. I guess their idea of training was a trial by fire. With five-hundred big ones in hand, I was told to not come back until I had that amount in drugs.

I won't forget the look on that one officer's face. From the way he carried himself, it's obvious that he thinks he's "the man" of this unit. His eyes were condemning when he saw me enter the building and mocking when I left. I guess he doesn't think pretty gals can do this sort of work.

Can't wait to wipe that smile off his face.

But I can't think of that right now. Armed with a freshly issued Glock, shining badge, fake ID, and my wits, I've got a job to do. And knowing what I know, I have a pretty good idea of where to start.

I've never handled drugs, let alone taken them, in my life. My family is strict Roman Catholic, and I would not even dare mention drugs in front of my folks. But growing up as a Hispanic in South Houston, I've seen people I know—people close to me—use them, take them, and sometimes even die by their hands. I've seen dealers, and I've seen their customers. I know what to look for and how to attract them to me.

Now, I'll use that knowledge to bust them.

***

My mother always told me to dress for success. However, today I'll be giving that advice a twist. The first thing I do after leaving the station is return home and dress the part. If you want to attract dealers, you've got to be dressed accordingly. During my teenage years and early adulthood, I've been approached by dealers out of the blue. Of course, I always turned them down. But what I learned is that your presentation can act as a magnet. Dress too nice and they won't approach you because they'll think you're square. Dress too down and they'll think you don't have the money. Somewhere between there is a nice medium.

Having changed in my apartment, I return to my car. Well, it's not really *my* car. It's my 'undercover car' as Captain Scott referred to it when he gave me the keys this morning. And just like me, it also looks the part. It's a beat down 1995 Dodge Avenger—the first model of its kind. This model came out my senior year in high-school and I had begged my parents to get me one, but they didn't see the value of getting me an overpriced car. That was five years ago, but it feels like yesterday. How ironic that it's the one given to me for my line-of-work.

The once bright red paint that I remember seeing in the ads is fading and the rims are more expensive than the car. The insides are a little torn up from the typical wear-and-tear that all vehicles experience. When this car was built four years ago, I'm sure it was a beauty. But now it's just a shadow of its former self.

Sitting in the driver's seat, I cannot help but admire my badge. It's silver with a picture of the great state of Texas in the middle. Or, as we Texans call it, the *nation* of Texas. Above it are the words 'Harris County' and higher than those words are the emboldened letters spelling 'Deputy'. 'Sheriff Dept' is written below the image of Texas. And last, but not least, is my name: Ana G. Rocha

I check my pistol before driving off. The worst thing that can happen today is for it to jam when needed. As I eject the clip and give it a once over, the satirical part of my mind plays the imaginary headline: *Undercover Officer Killed on First Day due to Jammed Gun.*

That would be a bummer.

A few minutes later, I pull up to a run-down convenience store. It's a beat down place with rusting walls and barred windows. A couple of the windows are cracked and one is broken. I guess that explains the reasoning for the metal bars. It's the stereotypical convenience store for an inner-city neighborhood and is definitely the kind of place you'd find the people I'm looking for.

There never is much of a spring in Texas and even less so in Houston. The seasons here are two months of winter and ten months of summer. It's only April, but it's already hot—some might call it scorching. Even in the clothes I'm wearing, I feel myself burning under the immense heat.

I thought I'd be nervous when the time for this came. But I'm not. My heart's beating like crazy, but I'm not afraid. Maybe I've rehearsed this so many times in my head that I know everything that'll happen by heart. Or maybe it's just the adrenaline kicking in. Either way, I'm not complaining.

Entering the store, I see him right away. He's lank and dressed like a bum. I figure that's his car parked two spots away from mine. It's just as beat up and unkempt as he is. The road tax sticker is two months expired too; however, that's not my concern today.

But I know better than to underestimate him.

My Glock is concealed and loaded. Not having a safety on it makes me a little uncomfortable, but I know how to use a gun. And I'm quick on the draw too.

I silently remind myself of my fake credentials: name, where I'm from, what I'm doing. The pessimistic part of my mind thinks I should have gone over everything at least one more time. I try to not stare at my target while keeping tabs on him through the corner of my eye. I go into the same aisle as him: the milk section. I pick a bottle out of the fridge. It reeks of expiration, but I act as if I'm reading the label. I have to wait for the perfect moment.

It all felt a bit surreal the whole way here. But now, being so close and knowing that the moment to strike it quickly approaching, reality sets in. My heart grows more excited with each passing second. It's almost the same thrill I would feel before a wrestling match in high school or before sparring in Taekwondo. The only difference is that this is much more intense.

Calm down. You've got this, Ana.

I take a deep breath, somewhat soothing my fast-beating heart. Feeling a gaze, I look up. My pretty eyes meet his reddish ones. However, it's only for a brief moment. Short enough to not be awkward, but long enough to get his attention. My gaze returns to the milk bottle as if I'm reading the label.

There's a long moment of silence… followed by another… and then a third. Each one is longer than the last. I barely stop my foot from tapping on the floor. Realizing that I'm crushing the milk bottle, I set it back down. But then I sense his approach. He slowly walks under the fluorescent lights until he's so close that I can smell his stench. I thought that my heart would be ready to burst out of my chest. Instead, it seems to stop.

This is it. With my lips curved into a slight smile, I let my gaze leave the bottle and come back to him.

***

"Ana, quite impressive work."

It's hardly past three when I returned to the station. When I came back, I held my head high and walked in like I owned the place. My stoic eyes completely ignored everyone else as I headed toward Captain Scott's office. From the looks other officers gave me, you would think I broke some sort of record. The same hands that carried the $500 now held brown bags full of the white powder I was asked to bring back. In fact, I got a little more than my money's worth.

Marching down the corridor, I managed to catch sight of that officer whose eyes had taunted me on my way out. Seeing me walk back in, the first thing he did was look away. But I felt his resentment. I even catch the name on his badge: Mark Davidson.

I'm sure it's a name I won't be forgetting anytime soon.

Now sitting across the desk from the police captain, I maintain my composure but can't stop smiling on the inside. He tries to keep his poise. However, it's obvious that he can hardly believe how quickly I returned. He skims all the paperwork I dropped on his desk. "...names, license plate numbers... on two different people?" He looks back at me. "I don't think I've ever seen anybody do this good on their first day."

"Well, now you have." Crap. That sounded better in my head. Hearing his compliment, I have the urge to jump with joy, but I somehow stop myself.

He slightly nods before sticking out his hand. "Congratulations, Officer Rocha."

I take his hand and firmly shake it.

"Welcome to the force."

***

After moving into my own place two months ago, the thrill of flying solo has already vanished. The apartment is in a nice gated complex and the neighbors are all good enough people. Living next door to me is a couple probably in their late twenties. I'm not sure what they do for a living, but the husband looks nerdy enough to be an engineer. Below me lives a cute little retired couple; the lady keeps tabs on all the neighbors while the husband could care less.

The apartment itself is pretty basic: two bedrooms, two bathrooms, a living room, a kitchen, and a small dining room. Not exactly the castle every girl dreams of but nothing for a single gal to be ashamed of either.

I use the smaller bedroom for myself. One wall of the bedroom is decorated with a few of my accolades. Among them are countless gold medals from my high school wrestling days, including the state championship, and my black belt from Taekwondo. I don't take any more formal martial arts classes but do practice my forms in the bedroom's open space.

The second bedroom is where things get more interesting. A board hangs from a bare wall. Tacked and taped all over the board is a web of facts. Arrows lead from one fact to the next—trails that would appear chaotic to anybody other than the person who drew them: me. In the center of all the notes and pictures is a photo of my smiling sister.

Coming through the front door and into the living room, I drop my bags on the sofa and lock the door behind me. The first thing I see is the picture on the coffee table. It was taken fifteen years ago when I was only seven-years-old. In the photo, I'm wrapped in my big sister's arms while we're out in some open fields. With her arms around me, she feverously tickles my sides. Our faces are filled with happiness and our eyes gleam with it. Joy radiates out of the frames. As she tickles me, I laugh so hard that I thought I'd die of it. And my laughter only amplifies hers.

It was… it was only a few days after this picture when she died.

***

The evening goes as can be imagined. Warm up a pre-cooked meal. Watch a little television. They're showing a re-run of the *X-Files*. I've never been able to get into that show, but my mother loves it. Seems a bit too convoluted to me. However, nothing else is on, so I watch the show about aliens and conspiracies.

It starts to rain as I turn in for the night. The lights flicker for a moment, but it's nothing out of the ordinary for when a storm hits. I'm not sure where the rainstorm came from since it was cloudless and blistering all day. But then again, this is Texas weather we are talking about. It's more bipolar than any woman I know.

The erupting thunder makes sleep a little harder tonight, and I find myself still awake when midnight rolls around. But when sleep finally does come, my dream returns me back to my job interview from a few weeks ago.

The chair is cold. So is the room. Sitting across the desk from the two interviewers, my heart races like never before. The room possesses no windows and the ceiling lights are blinding. It almost feels like an interrogation; the only thing missing is handcuffs.

I see that plump, red-headed woman's face. The threatening gaze from her green eyes shows that she is more of an intimidator and less of an interviewer. Even just the first syllable of her insulting voice gets under my skin. Part of me thinks that she does this all on purpose. "Ms. Rocha, you do realize how unorthodox it is to jump from being a jailor to a narcotics investigator? And then there's your young age. Most girls at twenty-two are graduating college, not going into narcotics."

I did not get a wink of sleep the night before the interview. I can't remember the last time that ever happened. But after having worked as a jailor for a long while, I know how to keep a straight face and how to never let others provoke an emotional response from me no matter how much of a nervous wreck I am inside. And all that experience comes to fruition in this bright and cold room. "Yes, ma'am, I do understand. But the recommendations from my supervisors demonstrate that during my time as a jailor I learned how to read people well—

especially the criminal element. I know how they act, talk, and think. But, most importantly, I know how to keep an upper-hand on them mentally. This will make me a valuable part of the narcotics unit."

"Perhaps it will. Your recommendations do show promise," the second interviewer comments. He leans forward a bit as he stares me right in the eyes. His voice is not as annoying, but his gaze is twice as bad. The lank man pauses, as if he is trying to be dramatic. "But seeing you here does raise a question."

This won't be good.

The red-head speaks again. "We've looked through the file of your sister's murder."

Is that even legal? I don't even know if these two people are actually officers or if they're just some random intimidators.

"Reading it, one cannot help but wonder. The drive-by shooters were caught and jailed shortly after the murder. However, there were rumors that the shooting was done due to a drug rivalry between two drug lords."

The second interviewer takes the reins of the interrogation. "Our undercover officers cannot be emotionally attached. They cannot have personal agendas. They need to do the job and do it well. Emotions affect decisions and bad decisions get people killed."

"So the question is," the red-head says, "Ms. Rocha, are you doing all this because of your sister? Are you trying to achieve some sort of personal satisfaction by putting your life on the line in this job? Because if that's the case, there's no place for you here."

You want to know the worst part? I don't know.

CHAPTER 2
DEADLY ENCOUNTERS

"You must be Ana."

Looking up from my desk, I see the plain-clothed officer walk into my office. He's a tall fellow, big enough to be an intimidating figure. I assume he's around ten-years-older than me and could easily lift me with just one arm. His badge hangs from a chain that goes around his neck. It's almost the same as my badge, except more weathered.

"I was last time I checked," I reply. Getting up, I meet him halfway and confidently shake his hand. He really does tower above me.

"Bryan Fulton." He politely smiles, but it's awkward enough to tell me that he doesn't do it often. "I've been assigned as your partner."

"Hope it's not something you'll be made to regret."

"Same here. But if it comes to that, one of us will probably be dead."

Was that supposed to be a joke? I'm not sure whether or not to laugh. He pauses as if expecting one, but the pause only makes the conversation more uncomfortable.

Looking away, Bryan reaches back and closes the door behind him. "I heard about what you did yesterday. First day on the job and two dealers bit your bait." He slightly shakes his head in amazement. "Wish I'd been there to see it."

I nod in appreciation. "So what's the word on me in the station?"

Bryan slightly shrugs. "Cap loves you. He even called a few of the vets in and bragged about you this morning. I've only ever seen him do that once before."

"How about the rest of the guys?"

"Well… the rest of the boys think you're a hard-ass."

11

My lips curve into a slight smile, having expected as much. "And what do you think?"

"I think you made them all jealous, especially Mark. He's the real hard-ass around here."

"I got that already."

I sit back in my chair while my new partner takes a seat across the desk. The office is not a big one, but it's roomy enough. Being in the middle of the building, there aren't any windows, except for the one on the door that lends a view of the hallway. Next to the door hangs a calendar that is turned to the current month and year: March 1999.

Just having moved into the office, there are not too many adornments. A bulky computer monitor rests on the wooden desk, its hard drive on the ground. A few pictures are scattered across the desk, showcasing my father, mother, brother, sister-in-law, and my late sister. Next to the photos is a stack of case files that were dropped on my desk just an hour ago. Behind me is a framed certificate with my name plastered on it. Under it are a few filing cabinets, but they are mostly empty at the moment. And on my door are the bolded words:

Ana Rocha
Narcotics Investigator

"So did Cap fill you in on everything?" Bryan asks, putting an end to all the small talk. Working with this guy is sure going to be a kicker.

"Everything from Pearland to the Galleria is our turf." Discreetly glancing at his hands that rest on the desk, I see that there's a small tan mark where his wedding ring would have been.

Bryan nods as his eyes scan the pictures. "Seems like you already know the spots where you'll find the best pickings."

"I grew up here so I heard things all the time."

"Drug dealers do seem to be more daring in Houston than in other places."

"Hopefully we can change that."

***

"So whad' ya want?"

We've not even been at the gas station for thirty seconds when Bryan starts talking to the guy at the pump next to ours. Apparently, gas stations and parking lots are the best places to find these dealers. The Hispanic man Bryan is targeting drives a beat-up, black Ford Contour whose rims and wheels are more expensive than the car itself. The target is dressed in the same manner as the two people I bought from my first day on the job.

Bryan did not give me any warning, other than telling me to stay in the car. He hopped out of the vehicle right after switching off the ignition and almost immediately started conversing with the target. With my head slightly turned, I can see the two, but try not to make it too obvious. I have my Glock in my lap in case anything happens. It's out of sight from the two men, but it's ready.

As soon as Bryan steps out of the car, he becomes a whole new person. His voice changes. His demeanor alters. His very aura is different. I don't know if even his own mother would recognize him. I stay in the car like he requests and watch him work flawlessly. He keeps the upper hand in the conversation and masterfully guides it in the direction that he wants.

And before I know it, Bryan has the man talking about… well, as he calls it, 'stones'.

"I just wanna know if you really got stones or not, brotha'?" Bryan replies.

"Depends on if you lookin' fo' some."

"If you got them, then I am."

"Well…" The man looks to his sides as if expecting to see something. "If that the case, then I do. How much you got?"

Bryan reaches into his pocket and pulls out a few bills. "This enough for you?"

The man greedily grins as he sees the money. After a long moment, he looks back up at Bryan. "I got you."

A few minutes later, Bryan is back in the car with me. And instead of gas, he has a bag of white powder with him. He does not say a word and quickly pulls out of the station. Right as he shuts the car door, his persona switches back to its real self. He acts as if nothing has happened and doesn't say a word about what he just did. Arriving back onto the main road, he still remains quiet. I'm not sure what to say or if he's even expecting me to say anything.

But once we are almost a minute into driving, he speaks without looking my way. "Write something down for me."

Opening the dashboard, I take out a notepad and pen.

"Name: Hugo Viel. License Plate number: CVN897. 5 feet 11 inches. Hair and eye color brown. Around 185 pounds."

I write it as fast as he says it. "Got it."

He doesn't reply.

There is another silence before I break it. "...so that was pretty great."

Bryan keeps his eyes focused on the road. His tone mirrors that of an annoyed older brother. "It was alright."

"Within five minutes you got him to sell you almost fifty dollars worth of goods. I think that's better than 'alright'."

"Remember these words Ana: the moment you start to think you're getting too good is the moment you are at most risk of getting killed. Don't get comfortable in this job—ever."

There is another awkward silence as I'm not sure what to say. We continue down the road, and I don't even ask where we're headed. I assume Bryan is heading over to another 'hot spot,' hoping to find another dealer.

For a few minutes, the only thing heard is the music of the car tires as they beat against the gravel. I get the feeling that this may be the first of many awkward and silent drives. There are not too many cars out at this time of day. It's almost two in the afternoon. Once the clock hits five, the roads will be clogged with Houston's rush hour traffic.

Finally, I look back at Bryan. "So... how did you know to target him?"

"His car, outfit, and demeanor."

"Profiling?"

"Is there a problem with that?"

I slightly shake my head.

"Give me a one-minute conversation with somebody, and I can tell you if they're selling or not. Do this long enough and spotting dealers becomes second nature."

"And how long have you been doing this?"

"Six years."

"All in Houston?"

He nods.

"Do you have a family here?"

There's no response. I guess that shouldn't surprise me.

A part of me wonders if the captain paired us together knowing that my personality is completely the opposite of Mr. Uptight here. Maybe he's back at the station laughing his head off at the thought of all this.

As I look away from Bryan, something tells me that this will be a long ride.

***

When I get home in the evening, the red light on my house phone is blinking. I feel like I'm having a heatstroke after being out under the Texas sun for what felt like a lifetime. Closing the door behind me, I make my way to the phone and hit the switch. My mother's calm voice suddenly fills the room.

"Hey baby, just calling to check up on you. Haven't seen you since you started the new job. I hope office work doesn't make you too busy to call your mom

anymore. But this weekend Ramon and Laura are coming over for lunch, and your father and I wanted to invite you over as well. Miss your smiling face around here. Umm…. just call me back when you get this message. Love you."

The line goes dead. I let out a sigh as I take a seat on the nearest couch. I toss my badge onto the coffee table and lean my head back, shutting my eyes. For obvious reasons, I have not mentioned the real nature of my work to my parents. Instead, I let them believe that I have a desk job and am a glorified receptionist at the police station. It does not take much to imagine why this deceit is necessary.

These past days have been so much that I nearly forgot the weekend starts the day after tomorrow. I've barely seen my parents since I moved out three weeks ago, but if my brother and sister-in-law are coming over, then I best be there as well.

That is if I survive tomorrow.

***

I barely arrive in my office when Bryan barges in.

"Ana, let's go."

I'm not surprised that he skips the pleasantries. Holding several photographs in his hands, he's dressed for undercover work. I snatch my Glock and badge from my desk. "What's going on?"

"An informant called. We've got work to do."

I follow him out of my office and down the illuminated corridor.

"We've got to make contact with four suspected dealers: Guel, James, Rodriguez, and Miller. These four people have been on our watch list and we finally caught a break on their whereabouts." Bryan hands me two of the photographs. "My informant told me where each of them will be from ten 'til noon today morning."

As we continue down the corridor, we pass several other men and women—some officers and some not—but I pay them no heed. I take a look at the photos and see two headshots. One displays a

Caucasian male. A long scar runs down his left cheek. The second shows a Hispanic male, his face hinting at his heavy figure.

"We'll have to split up to get them all in time. You'll go after Guel and Miller. I'll go after the other two."

"Why don't we just send teams to pick them up?"

"We need hard evidence first."

Bryan and I are nearly at the station's front doors.

"Make contact with them. If you can, buy from them right now and then tag them. A team will pick them up later. If not, set up a meet for later and we'll go from there." He pauses for a moment. "These are four people we've been after for a while, Ana. You want your chance to prove yourself as an officer? This is it."

A part of me knows that splitting up is a little unorthodox, but there is no other option given the small window of opportunity. And I am sure Bryan got the captain's permission for all this. "Got it."

***

"You must be Miller."

It hasn't been two minutes since I pulled up to the convenience store when I start talking to him. The shop is a rundown joint. Half the windows are cracked, chipped, or even broken. It's just off the main road and is in full view of any cars that may pass by. Based on all the signs hanging from the store windows, you'd think that all they sold here was alcohol. Miller and another man are lounging outside the store's front. I imagine that this is their turf. Sitting on lawn chairs, they each have a bottle in hand. The scar running down Miller's face is just like the photograph showed. Probably got it from his line of work.

It's blistering hot today, and the sun beats against the back of my neck. However, I know that the heat is not causing even half my sweating. My jet black hair is tied back into a long ponytail. A sleeveless top covers my torso while my legs wear a pair of shorts. My Avenger's running engine makes it hard for my voice to be heard as I stand next to the vehicle.

Miller looks my way for a few moments. After a while, he glances back at his lackey before smirking at me. His voice is just as I imagined: a confident shell with a cowardly inside. I've heard it plenty of times from inmates to recognize the type. "Well, honey, that depends on who's asking."

"I'm new in town." Unbeknownst to both these men, I have my loaded Glock in my back pocket. "I need a new source."

"Source for what?"

"My neighbor said she gets her stones from you. Says you're the best game in town around these parts."

He raises one of his eyebrows. "Neighbor? What's your neighbor's name?"

I annoyingly put my hand on my car's top. "Are you Miller or not?"

He glances back at his friend for a moment. The friend is a tall fellow and possesses devilish eyes. His sleeveless shirt and shorts show his toned arms and legs. It seems like the two of them are communicating through their eyes, but I cannot figure out what it is. Finally, Miller's gaze returns to me. "How much you got?"

"Hundred fifty."

"Minimum of two hundred for a new client."

I know he's lying through his teeth and just trying to see how much I really have on me. But I play along. "Aight... I got that on me."

"You just said—"

"I have another fifty in the car."

There is another uneasy silence before Miller breaks it. But when he does speak, his smirk grows. "Meet me behind the store. We're too out in the open here."

***

I drive my car out back and see the two waiting for me next to the shop's back door. There aren't any windows along the store's back wall and no other places where people could spy on what happens here. Perfect place for an exchange. I keep my car running as I step out of it. My pistol is still concealed.

Holy—I can't believe that I'm not dreaming. 10 minutes ago I was driving down the road. Now I'm staring a suspected criminal in the face.

I'm not far from the two of them. Five yards at the most. More than close enough to smell their stench. As soon as I'm out of the car, I get an uneasy feeling in my heart. But it's too late to turn back now without blowing this whole operation. I've already tagged their license plates. Just make the buy and get out of here.

"I don't see no bags," I annoyingly comment upon noticing Miller's empty hands.

"It's inside. Money first."

Keeping my gaze on him and his lank lackey, I produce a few bills from my pocket. But I immediately put them away after he gets a look at them.

"Money first," he repeats. "Then the stones."

"You think I'm an idiot? Show me the goods first."

Miller stares at me for what feels like a long time. He's trying to intimidate me, but unluckily for him, it's to no avail. "You want the goods, girl?" He looks at his henchman. "Here they are."

The look in his eyes… something feels off. Something feels way too—

No!

The lackey suddenly leaps at me. He's holding a switchblade! And it's aimed at my stomach!

My mind doesn't realize what is happening. But my instincts do. Impulsively, I sidestep the attack and quickly register everything. As he stumbles past me, I violently crash my elbow into his face, breaking his nose and making him let out a painful grunt.

I whip out my loaded Glock as Miller comes at me with a knife of his own. He's close—too close for me to get a shot. Miller swings his blade, forcing me to duck down. His free hand grabs the barrel of my gun before his forearm crashes into my jaw. I feel blood running out of my nose as his boot strikes my stomach. I quickly stumble a few feet back. I lose my gun, and it slides underneath my car.

I regain my balance as the two men rush me, switchblades in hand.

Come on, Ana. Get control of yourself. Remember everything. Don't get emotional. Predict and attack—predict and attack.

Miller is the closer of the two. With the right side of his body cocked back, his right hand holds his blade. He'll lead with it. A quick glance at the lackey tells me that he's waiting for his boss to make the first move. Blood running from his broken nose, the lackey keeps his eyes on Miller. Once his boss attacks, the lackey will follow to finish me off.

Or so he thinks. My heart is racing—my mind runs wild. But I control my breathing like I was taught to do.

Wait for it. The best offense is a good defense. Wait for it. Let him make the first move. He'll come at you with the knife. Ignore the blood and block out the pain. Concentrate on him. Patience... patience... patience.

There is a moment of calm. Then Miller makes his move.

He lunges at me with his knife. But I already saw it coming and sidestep him with ease. The blade runs right by me, mere inches from my ribs. As he misses, I step up into him.

Attack with precision. Don't go for the finishing blow. Just stun him to even out the odds.

My open palm strikes Miller right below the diaphragm, knocking the wind out of him.

"Uuuff—"

I bring my knee up. It nails Miller right between his legs. Before he can even fully register the pain, I powerfully strike his skull with my elbow. He spits out a stream of blood as I shove him onto the concrete ground.

Turning around, I dodge the lackey's knife by inches, leaving it to cut air. Grabbing his wrist, I yank him in close, while keeping my free hand's palm open.

Make this strike count. Finish him before Miller regains his composure.

Forcing him close enough, my palm mercilessly nails his trachea. His eyes widen. His whole body goes numb for a few moments as he lets out a gurgle. Any harder and it may have killed him. The knife falls from his hand and loudly lands on the ground. Grabbing him by his hair, I smash his face against the metallic hood of my car with everything I've got. His face fills with blood and his unconscious body collapses.

I waste no time and twirl around. Miller comes back at me with his knife. I duck and his blade passes right over my skull. Coming up, I grab his wrist and twist his arm while powerfully kicking him in the stomach.

Finish him quickly. No telling how many others he might have here.

He howls in pain as he lets go of the knife and stumbles back. Taking advantage, I snatch up the switchblade and spring onto him. I ruthlessly jam the blade right into his calf, making him fall to his knees as he howls in even more pain. Seizing his hair, I raise my other fist and bring it down. The blow draws blood. It comes down again. More blood. Again.

Still holding him by his head, I bring up my knee and shove his head toward it. They both collide with enough force to be heard at the front of the store. I let go of the bloodied body and it falls to the ground.

But there is no time to think. Right as his unconscious body hits the concrete, I hear something behind me.

The fight's not over yet.

Turning around, my entire vision is engulfed by a fist a moment before it slams into my face.

Clap!

I stumble back, completely dazed. Without seeing the man, the back of my mind screams that it is the storekeeper. He must have been in on this. His powerful fist strikes my skull again, and I stagger back before falling onto a knee.

Protect your skull, Ana! Whatever you do—

Still on a knee, I shield my head with my arms just as he sends his boot. It smashes against my forearms, numbing them with pain. But better them than my head. My forearms immediately catch another kick. Then a third.

Let's move, Ana. You're not going to let some punk kill you. Not some low-life filth like this. You're better than him. You've got the badge, not him.

I block another kick.

Wait. Patience. Wait… attack when there's an opening.

He sends his next kick. This time, I don't block it. Moving on pure instinct, I firmly grab his boot mid-flight. Stepping up, I shove him backward as I rise to my feet. Blood is streaming down my face from multiple cuts on the sides of my skull. My head is spinning and my body aches, but the adrenaline keeps the pain at bay, while my focus keeps my mind in the game.

I finally get a good look at my foe as I come at him. He's big. Strong. And this isn't his first brawl.

But now he's going to get a load of me.

The dark-skinned man keeps his brutish gaze aimed at me. He raises both powerful fists up like a boxer. With his right leg cocked back, I know he's right-handed. That's his power arm, and that's what I need to look out for. Let him throw that and then get in close. Take away the advantage of his height and play to my strengths.

He sends a jab with his left fist, but I sidestep it. It comes again, but I avoid it by stepping back. The brute throws it a third time, but I again easily sidestep it.

That's right big fella', get annoyed. Get angry that you can't hit a woman. Come at me with your power arm, and I'll end this.

With a roar, he wildly sends his right fist and leaves himself exposed. I duck to avoid the strike and step up into him, no more than a foot away. I swiftly kick him right in the crotch, but I don't show him any mercy. My right fist smashes against his face. I follow through with my elbow, fist, and elbow again, all in quick succession. He may be stronger, but I know how to focus my energy. And with each blow, he spits out blood.

With him dazed, I plunge my knee into his stomach, making him keel over. Grabbing him by his bald head, I sling him onto the ground. He crashes headfirst onto the pavement. His eyes tell me that I almost have him.

Finish him, Ana.

Running up to him, I give him a quick kick to the head, knocking him out cold.

CHAPTER 3
GROWING PAINS

What just happened?

My breaths are quick. My heart is on the verge of bursting. Pain rings through me. Streams of blood run from the sides of my head and down my cheeks, while cuts, sweat, and bruises are scattered across my body.

A part of me still can't believe what occurred. It all happened so fast, and my mind refuses to register this as reality. It tries to convince me that, at any moment, I'll wake up from this nightmare. At any moment, I'll realize that this is all just a bad dream.

But that doesn't happen. This is reality.

Thousands of thoughts clog my mind as I stare down at my work. All three men are out cold. As bad of a beating as I took, it is nothing compared to what I dished out. None of them will be getting up anytime soon. As I focus on the largest thug, I can't believe that I actually took them all out, especially this one. God must have really been on my side.

The memory of the fight races through my head, every movement replayed. The brawl moved so quickly that I never even had a chance to soak anything in. Every action, reaction, and thought was purely instinctive.

Luckily, those instincts were good enough to keep me alive.

Even with the imminent danger gone, my heart rate won't slow down. And neither will my breathing. With the adrenaline kicked in, there's no stopping it now.

Stepping over the unconscious bodies, I crouch down and see my Glock underneath my Avenger, barely within arms-length. I reach toward it, feeling its grip brush against the tips of my fingers before I painfully pull it toward me. Rising up to my feet, I quickly make sure that the gun is not jammed. I pay one last glance at the largest thug. He probably received a decent concussion, and his head is bleeding worse than mine is. But he'll live.

Turning away from them all, I make my way toward the shop's heavy backdoor. The sun seems hotter than ever as it beats against my back. I thought it would be impossible, but my heart is pounding even faster now as my mind quickly imagines the worst things that could be waiting for me inside.

But I've never been one to give in to fear.

With my gun raised and aimed straight ahead, I step up and forcefully kick the metallic door. It swings on its hinges with a loud screech before fully opening. My finger is on my gun's trigger. There's no safety on the weapon, and I can't control my arm from trembling a bit. Not hesitating, I charge in with my weapon readied, quickly looking and aiming to either side. The shop appears empty... at least initially. It's completely silent, almost to the extent of giving it an eerie presence. The fluorescent lights are flickering and there's a foul stench in this place that I can't recognize.

I ignore it and make a quick sweep of the aisles, just to make sure that I am alone in here. I keep my weapon raised as I do so. The racks are mostly full of alcohol, snacks, drinks, and candy. But no people. My only companions are a couple of cockroaches scurrying around and another few that are dead on their backs. Glock still in hand, I cautiously walk over to the phone next to the cash register. I look behind the counter and find it vacant as well. No fourth hostile anywhere. Thank God.

Letting out an inner sigh of relief, I slowly holster my weapon. My head has finally stopped spinning. With a few quick hits, I dial a number and put the phone to my ear. It quickly rings twice before a female voice answers the other end.

"South Houston Police Station."

"This is Officer Rocha." Speaking into the phone, I do my best to mask the unrelenting pain. And for the most part, I think it works. "I've been assaulted by three suspects but have them all in custody. I need a unit sent to bring them in. I also believe that the convenience store I'm at may house a stash of drugs in the back. I need a warrant to search it."

She doesn't hesitate, and her tone doesn't change. *"Where are you, officer?"*

I tell her the address.

"Units will be there shortly and Judge Bradley will be contacted about the warrant. Stay on the scene and keep the perimeter contained until then."

"Will do."

"Are you hurt?"

"Only my pride."

"Do you require medical attention?"

"…not for anything major."

I hang up the phone and slowly stagger toward the bathroom. Holding my Glock with both hands, I again raise the gun and keep it steadied straight ahead. The closer I get to the restroom, the stronger this place's foul odor grows. But I'm not surprised by it.

Coming to the door, I raise my leg and forcefully kick it open. It flies on its hinges before loudly crashing against the wall. I move in and do a quick scan of the single-person restroom. There's nobody here. Still quivering a bit, I again holster my weapon.

The bathroom's lights also flicker. The walls possess countless cracks, and the mirror is partially broken. I look at the reflection staring back at me and a part of me thinks I'm hallucinating. I've been feeling the blood, but I didn't think that it was this bad. I look like Rocky Balboa after a boxing match, only a little uglier. If someone sees me like this, they'd think that I just came out of a war.

Then again, that is not too far from the truth.

Reality quickly sets in. I violently pull out countless paper towels from the dispenser. Turning on the water faucet, I lightly wet them with the dirty water. Using what minimal training I have about treating wounds, I apply pressure to the two largest cuts on the sides of my head. They sting for a quick moment, causing me to wince, but I don't stop. I feel the towels start to slowly get soaked by the blood seeping out of the wounds—my blood—and the more I think about it, the more lightheaded I start feeling. Closing my eyes, I try to not think of the wounds. Instead, I take several deep breaths to clear my head and to get my heart rate under control like I was taught to do in Taekwondo.

The first few breaths don't do much. With my eyes shut, all I see are the countless times I was nearly killed only minutes ago. I see the murderous faces of Miller and his merciless goons. Their eyes are filled with evil and greed. I remember feeling the knives cutting only a hair-length away from my skin. I remember my head spinning so bad that I could barely think straight enough to defend myself.

But… somehow I made it.

The next few breaths clear my head of these thoughts. The more pressure I place onto the wounds, the slower the bleeding seems to become. But I keep my eyes lightly closed and continue to control my breathing. I don't know how long it takes, but I doubt it's more than a handful of minutes. My heart rate finally comes under control and the bleeding is now minimal at best.

Opening my eyes, I toss the bloodied paper towels into the trash bin. I lean my palms onto the cracked sink's sides as I take one more good look at my beaten face. And as I look at the reflection of my brown eyes, all I can think of is one thing: I survived. I made it through. I took whatever those animals dished out and I gave them more.

…I survived.

***

The police arrive at the scene a few minutes after I walk back outside. One right after the other, four patrol units come speeding around to the back of the store, their sirens deafeningly blaring. Arriving at a halt, eight officers rush out with their guns drawn and readied. They are quick in their work as each officer knows their assignment before they even step out of the car. All three suspects—still unconscious—are soon in handcuffs. Miller and his lackey are thrown into the back of one patrol car while the larger brute is put into a second vehicle. By the time they wake up, they'll be on their way to the station. And Miller will have to tell everyone that he was beaten by a woman.

I'm sure that'll hold up well in prison.

Judge Bradley was apparently quick in issuing the search warrant. There was more than enough probable cause for him to sign off right away. Four of the officers immediately barge into the store with their guns drawn. Two do a quick sweep of the building one more time to make sure no remaining hostiles are lurking around; the other two carry out the warrant's orders. Minutes later, they come out with two crates in their hands. Even from where I stand, I can smell the drugs. Their expressions suggest that this type of score is far above the average bust.

Another uniformed officer sits me down on the trunk of his car as he examines my wounds. I doubt he's had any more formal medical training than I have, but at least he acts like he knows what he's doing. Maybe he's done this sort of thing before. I hope it's not something that is too commonplace on the job.

He uses a first-aid kit to try to sterilize the cuts in an effort to ensure that they don't get any kind of infection. While he works on me, another cop takes down my report detailing all the events that happened. I don't think he can really fathom that I took down all three of the hostiles without a weapon. He soon leaves, but the officer working on me continues to do so for a few minutes.

The 'medic' keeps a piece of cloth pushed up against the cut on the right side of my head for a few moments before finally breaking the silence. "Keep this cloth pressed up against the wound."

I take the cloth from him and follow his instructions.

"Cuts aren't too deep and will heal in time. Doesn't look like you need to go through the fun of stitches."

"I'm in tears already."

He slightly smiles at the sarcasm. "You've had quite a day it seems."

"I hope not all of them are this exciting. When I woke up today, I was not planning on getting nearly killed so that some punks could score an easy couple of hundred bucks."

"Rest assured, it was not a day wasted. None of those three will be seeing freedom anytime soon. Assault of an officer with deadly force and possession of over ten kilos of cocaine is enough to put anybody away for a long time."

"Hopefully long enough to make them rethink their lives." I glance down for a moment. The vision of Miller's knife nearly cutting me down flashes in my mind's eye. He was willing to gut me just for a few bucks. What kind of man does that? "It was a bit too close for comfort."

The officer reassuringly puts his hand on my shoulder. "You made it out and that's what's important. Not every officer I've known who's gotten into a scuffle like this is around anymore to say the same thing."

I'm not entirely sure how to respond to that. Looking at the man's badge, I read his golden name tag. "Thanks for the help, William."

"Make sure you let a doctor have a good look at you."

"I will."

He takes a step back and turns away as I rise to my feet. I make my way over to the officer who took down my report. He's standing next to his car's open door. Seeing me coming, he politely smiles.

"What's the word back at the station?" I ask.

"They're all glad you made it, Ana."

I take another glance at the scene all around me. Blue-clad officers are all over the grounds as they each carry out their assignments. There are plenty of officers here, but I notice the one who is missing. I'm sure the station paged my *oh-so-amazing* partner and told him what had happened. But, not entirely surprisingly, he's failed to show up even after hearing his partner was attacked.

"Does Bryan know?"

The officer nods. "I spoke to him a moment ago. Told him everything that happened."

"What did he say?"

"Well…" He hesitates, looking away for a quick second. "He was upset."

"About what?"

"About you—well, as he put it… about you not following protocol and costing the entire department time and resources. He said you were 'reckless'."

"*Reckless?*"

After a pause, the officer slightly nods.

Not exactly the best beginning of a partnership.

***

Outside of the soreness, my body and mind are fully functioning by the time I return home to change out of my clothes and take a shower, not wanting to show up at the police station looking like a post-fight kickboxer. But I don't bother to stop by the hospital before arriving back at the station. That can wait. The bruises and cuts on my legs are covered by a pair of jeans, leaving only the marks on my arms and head visible.

I aggressively push through the station's front doors and make my way to my office. I get a few stares, but nobody says anything to me and I disregard their gawking. I am only focused on one thing—or to be more exact, one person.

As I continue down the corridor, somebody comes in my path only a few feet away. Mark Davidson steps out of his office, obviously for a stretch, but stops when he sees the cuts on my face.

"What happened to—"

Without a word, I forcefully shove him out of my way. He staggers back into his office, barely able to keep himself from falling over. I don't even look his way or hesitate as I move past him. My office door is slightly open, signaling that somebody is in there, and my gut tells me just who it is.

Bryan is sitting across from my vacant chair looking down at his hand. He was apparently waiting for me. But his head slowly turns to face me as I loudly slam the door shut. His eyes don't show any concern or happiness to see me alive. However, before I can say a word, he's the one to speak. "We lost Guel."

For a moment, confusion replaces my anger. "…what?"

"You were supposed to meet Miller first before making contact with Guel. We've lost Guel and Lord knows when we'll get another crack at him." He pauses. "Or did you forget all that?"

There's an awkward silence in the room. But it is just the calm before I explode. "I almost *died* out there and all you're concerned with is some punk!? What the hell is wrong with you—"

Bryan suddenly stands up. He towers above me and that stops me in my tracks. "Rule number one, Ana: never lose your gun. Rule number two: never let the suspect choose the meeting point. You broke *both* rules today and that's why you almost got killed."

For a moment, I'm at a loss for words.

"You should have been the one calling the shots, Ana, not Miller. You knew that, but you still went along with his meeting point. Lucky for you, God was on your side today and has given you another chance. I suggest you make the most of it and learn from today. Because *your mistake* has ensured that another dealer is still out on the streets. A dealer who has already destroyed too many lives. And how many more lives will Guel destroy before we get another chance at him? How much has your mistake cost the people you swore to protect?"

I have no answer.

Bryan slowly walks by me. "So don't come in here blaming anybody but yourself for what happened out there. If you're looking for somebody to be angry at, then look in the mirror."

Before I can even register what he said, Bryan is gone.

***

After his departure, I'm speechless for a little while. With Bryan's words in my mind, I go to the hospital like suggested and have the doctor take a look at me. But even there, I can't think of anything other than what Bryan said. I hardly even catch anything the doctor says.

Eric—the doctor—cleans a few of my cuts more thoroughly than William did. But like William's prediction, he says I don't need any stitches and sends me on my way as quickly as I arrived. I'm surprised he doesn't ask me how I received the beating. I drive back to the station almost on autopilot. By the time I get there, the emotions of anger cast a shadow on Bryan's words.

I don't know what Captain Scott was doing before I barge into his office. He may have been on the phone with the sheriff himself, but I can care less at the moment. I open his door without knocking before I commandingly close it behind me. He immediately looks up from his paperwork.

Cap politely smiles, unfazed. "You've had quite the day, Ana. I'm glad to see you visited a doctor."

"Sir, we need to talk."

Hearing my tone, he slightly leans back in his chair. "What about, Ana?"

"Bry—my partner. I don't think it's going to work out."

"And why's that?"

"He's…"

"Uncaring?" His calm tone hints that he expected this visit.

I slightly nod.

"He's been like that for some time now." Cap fully leans back in his chair, but he keeps his eyes on me. "It tends to happen to people who go through what he did. I've seen it happen to countless officers like him. But I did think that you'd last at least a week before coming to me."

I almost don't want to ask the next question. "...what happened?"

"You should go and see for yourself. I'd advise you to take a look at his office and then at his hand. See if your deductive skills can figure it out. If you still want a new partner after that, I'll see what I can do."

"...alright."

"You've been through a lot for your first week." Cap returns to his original posture. "Take next week off if you want. Maybe you can reassess if this is the type of career you really want."

Not entirely knowing what to say, I turn around to leave.

"And Ana..."

I look back at Cap. "Yes, sir?"

"Next time: knock."

***

The captain's words remain at the forefront of my mind when I finally make it home. The low sun is almost touching the horizon as it paints the sky in a mix of red and orange. Walking in through my apartment's front door, I can't focus on anything as I replay Cap's parting advice. A good part of my mind is rethinking my career choice. And by rethinking, I mean seriously considering the options here.

When I went to Bryan's office after speaking to the captain, the room appeared vacant and the door was securely locked. Turns out that Bryan had just left to meet some informants and would be gone for a while. I had no interest in waiting around for him.

Finally back in the confines of my apartment, I no longer need to keep up this alpha female act. The adrenaline that pumped through my veins is all but gone, leaving me completely exhausted. The soreness is at its worst now and rings from every corner of my body. Entering the larger bedroom that holds the web of facts, I slump onto the floor like a sack of dead weight. My elbows rest on my thighs as my head hangs low.

My gaze focuses on the maze hanging from the wall opposite of me. I focus on the photo of my sister at the center of it.

After a long moment, I shut my eyes and see the vile face that tried to kill me. I smell the foul odor that radiated off Miller and his wolves. At first, there is absolute peace in the room as my mind's eye witnesses the fight once more.

But it is merely the serenity before the storm.

Suddenly, my body begins to uncontrollably tremble as the scene is again replayed in my mind. Goosebumps form all across my arms and legs, and it is not from the cold. Before I even realize it, my eyes swell with tears, and streams are flooding down my cheeks. My irrepressible sobs fill the apartment, loud enough to be heard outside. And the more I cry, the more I realize just how close I was to dying. I finally realize what really happened.

In this moment, sitting here all alone in this empty room with no companion other than my thoughts and the web of facts that has driven me for so long, I finally realize that only a few inches separated me from death at the hands of Miller's knife. I realize that another human being tried to kill me. Another person deemed my life less valuable than a wad of dirty, green paper.

And he was willing to murder me in cold blood for it.

No matter how hard I try, I cannot stop weeping or quivering as fear courses through every vein. It goes into my very heart and drowns out anything else. I can't do anything to stop it. I'm powerless... completely powerless. It's as if I'm the little girl again.

The little girl who just learned that her sister was dead. The little girl who lost her best friend. The little girl who suddenly felt all alone.

Except... this time, I really am alone.

CHAPTER 4
THE VOW

Like the nights I have come to know, I spend this one alone. But the chaos in my mind keeps slumber far from me until an hour before sunrise. And when dawn arrives, I have all but forgotten about the family get-together. Fortunately, my mother calls me an hour before it starts. Sleeping on the long couch, I almost fall off when the loud ringing suddenly cuts through the silent room.

The phone call wakes me up from a hazy dream. Luckily, by the time I answer the phone I am able to hide my weariness and make her believe that I was in the process of getting ready. She buys the lie. Hanging up, I make a quick dash to the bathroom.

The first things I check are the cuts on my face. To no surprise, they're still there and can be seen just as easily as the day before. There's no possible way to explain them without arousing suspicion. But by casually letting my long hair down, the cuts are covered up. Thank God for that. I take a quick shower to freshen up, hoping to smell like a lady who has a desk job and not one who spends most of her hours out in the Texas heat. The cuts still sting a little when the water crashes against them, but I ignore the pain.

I wear a pair of white jeans and a long-sleeve pink tunic to cover all the small cuts and bruises on my arms and legs. Had the coming day's festivities been out at the park instead of at my parents' home, these clothes would have been hell to wear. One final look in the mirror confirms that everything needing to be concealed is.

And with that, I am off.

***

My parents own a nice-sized home. Some may even call it a mansion. Daddy came to this country as an 18-year-old man with hardly a cent to his name and just a single suitcase of clothes. He was the true blue immigrant with nothing to claim his own except for the American Dream. He started off as a construction worker. When he had enough money, he married my mom and brought her over to the states. It was not long after then that he started his own lawn care business around the time my sister, Angela, was born. And by the time I was brought into this world, his business had expanded to include two car washes, a motel, and a couple of convenience stores.

I'm the last one to arrive. As I drive past the open gate at the end of the long driveway, I see my brother's bright golden Lexus already on the driveway. It's parked right behind my mom's red Cadillac and my father's jet black BMW.

The home is by far the biggest in the neighborhood. And in an area like this, that is certainly saying something. Standing three stories high, the red-bricked building is visible for miles around. It's surrounded on each side by two acres before the property ends. Ancient trees provide plenty of shelter on the lot. In one tree is a treehouse I grew up playing in. Tied to the thick branch of another tree is a set of swings that my sister would push me on.

The long driveway goes from the gate to the estate's front door. There are two white pillars on either side of the large front door that hold up the second floor's balcony. The white window shutters and white designs on the exterior of the house complement the red bricks perfectly. This place is the definition of a million-dollar home.

As my vehicle comes to a halt, the back of my mind is worrying that my disguise won't hold up and that my parents will see right through my lies if they start asking questions. Or even worse, they'll catch sight of my wounds. Stepping out of my vehicle, I make my way to the heavy wooden door. It opens before I even ring the doorbell. Standing on the other side is my sweet 'ole mother. My mom is as nice as they come.

Quick to forgive and slow to blame. She didn't speak any English when she first came to the states and had to put up with a lot because of it. I imagine that those experiences gave her such a tolerant heart.

The first thing she does is envelop me in a hug. It's the type of embrace only a mother can give. And without even thinking, I reciprocate the gesture.

"Hey, baby."

"Sorry to keep you waiting, mama."

She seems to hold me for a long time. Long enough for our heartbeats to almost sync with one another. But, she finally lets go and I'm able to enter the house. "Everyone's out back."

I follow her into the foyer. There is a circular staircase that leads to the second and third floors. The wood of the railings and steps matches the floor's polished wood. To the left is a home office and to the right is one of the house's two dining rooms. But straight ahead is the back door.

Within moments of me stepping in, a small brown mutt comes charging around the corner and toward me, barking as it does. Its curly fur bounces in the air as it runs full speed ahead. For a moment, I think that it will ram right into me. But it suddenly stops at my feet. With a quick sniff of my toe, it briskly turns around and trots off without a second glance.

"Glad to see you too, Chica," I mutter with a smile.

The backdoor leads to a large, covered patio. There are plenty of black, comfortable lounge chairs out here—close to twelve or so. To go along with the chairs are several matching tables. Not far from the patio rests a large swimming pool surrounded by mosquito netting. Around the pool are a few pool chairs.

Even from inside, I heard the Spanish music blasting through the outside speakers. It's a family tradition for cookouts, and I doubt my brother can even operate the grill without these melodies. As soon as I step outside, I hear Ramon's voice. "*Hola, hija.*"

"Hey, bro."

Ramon stands behind the grill at the edge of the covered patio. With a spatula in hand, he's dressed in a pair of worn-out shorts, flip-flops, and a stained t-shirt. He's even slowly wiggling to the music as he mouths the words. He looks like the stereotypical Mexican cook. He's a big fella with an even bigger heart. Whenever I see him, I am reminded of how being a minister is the perfect job for him.

I haven't even been here for two seconds when my sister-in-law seemingly comes out of nowhere to give me a hug. "So good to see you, Ana."

"You too, Laura." I see my dad sitting on a lounge chair not far from my brother. "How are you doing, dad?"

"Seeing you makes my day brighter every time." He smiles at me as he reaches into the cooler at his feet.

"You're as charming as ever."

Daddy tosses a can of cold soda toward me and I easily catch it with one hand. "Saved that one just for you."

I take a seat at the table across from him and am joined on either side by my mother and sister-in-law. The covering protects us from the endless early summer heat, while the fans keep our little sanctuary cool. But the aromas of the burgers and hot dogs Ramon is grilling are to die for.

"It's only been a few weeks since you've moved out and you've already lost weight," my mom almost immediately comments.

"I don't have anyone with me to make me overeat."

She lightly pushes my shoulder in jest. "It's better for a person to be healthy than skinny."

I look over at my dad and respond, "I think daddy's the proof of that."

Laura and my mom stifle their laughs, but Ramon doesn't hold back as he continues working at the grill. My dad looks over at him and speaks with a grin plastered on his face. "You're in the same boat as me so I wouldn't be laughing too hard over there."

"Same boat but different ends."

Shaking his head, my dad looks back at me. "How's the new job, Ana?"

No sooner does my dad ask the question that it happens. The image of Miller's blood-thirsty eyes flashes through my mind. And it is followed by Bryan's condemning words. The mix of fear and uncertainty that possessed me the night before suddenly runs rampant in my heart. But taking an internal deep breath, I display no signs of the flashbacks as I slightly shrug. The pleasant smile on my face remains there. "Just as exciting as you'd think a desk job will be."

"I'm just glad that you're not working around that jail anymore. But I still don't see why you felt like you needed to get a desk job at the police department. I could've given you a desk job at our company if you wanted. Better yet, I could've let you manage one of the businesses."

I can't believe how easily I just lied to my own father's face. And even more, I can't believe that he and everyone around me just bought the lie. "I just wanted to try something new, dad. I worked at the family company all through high school and just wanted to work somewhere where I'd get the 'real' job environment experience."

"I think after seeing the 'real' job environment, you'll really start to appreciate the family company more. Most workplaces aren't like what your mother and I built." He takes a deep breath as he glances down at his lap for a quick moment. "But hopefully you don't want to stay there too long. I'm getting too old to run this company by myself."

"You're not even fifty-five dad. I hardly consider that old."

"Let's see if you're still saying that when you're fifty."

"Besides, you have Ramon to take over the company."

"I would, but he's too much of a pastor now to want to run a company. Between that and running his non-profit, he doesn't have time to learn the ropes. He's been on four humanitarian trips this year." My dad slightly smiles. "I'm not sure what he's done that he needs to repent so much."

My brother laughs as he makes his way toward us. In his hands are two plates, each with a cheeseburger and two hotdogs. The closer he comes, the more my taste buds start craving for the flavors as the aromas dance all around me. The food is sizzling hot as the cheese melts into the meat. He places the plates in front of me and my dad. "The first one was for my sins, dad, but the other three were for all yours!"

We lightly laugh before my dad speaks again. "But seriously, Ana, how long do you think you'll be working there?"

"I don't know." There's more truth to that than any of them realize. In fact, there's more truth to that than even I know. Because like Cap said, I may not be going back there ever. After what happened yesterday, a part of me doesn't think I'd live to see my one-month anniversary, let alone a year. As I sit there in my family's presence, Cap's words once again replay in the back of my head. I hear him again as he tells me to rethink if I really am capable of doing this.

"Ana?"

I'm suddenly brought back to reality by Laura's words. My sister-in-law's hand is on top of mine, causing me to quickly look at her.

"Did you hear what I said?"

"Sorry. My mind was somewhere else."

She and Ramon exchange a glance before she looks back at me. "Well, we have some exciting news to tell you. Mom and dad already know this."

Ramon takes the reins of the conversation. "Me and Laura are having a baby."

...what? For a moment, I am speechless. But then my eyes suddenly widen with surprise. "Congratulations!"

My words are quickly followed by a round of hugs for my brother and his wife. But for some reason, I don't feel the joy everyone else experiences. I don't know why, but my heart feels hollow as I see the excitement in my family's eyes and hear their laughter. But I put up a good face.

As can be imagined, the rest of the lunch is spent talking about the upcoming baby, even though the child is still months away. But the honest truth is that I'm glad it goes that way. I'd rather everyone talk about anything else other than my new job. The last thing I want to tell them is that I'm seriously considering leaving the job after only a few days of working there. That would just lead to more questions than I have the answers to right now.

In fact, right now my mind has more questions of its *own* than it has the answers to.

***

The whole way home, I feel sick to my stomach. I don't know exactly why. For the hours I was with my family, I was around so much happiness. Talking about the upcoming baby made everything seem so jovial. But from the moment I step out of my parents' abode, I just want to throw up. Maybe it's because I lied to my family's faces without even blinking. Each and every one of them. I did it without a second thought and without hesitating.

Or maybe it's because I am even more confused than ever about what I need to do. If I don't turn back, I risk getting myself killed. And even worse, I risk crushing my family's happiness. My parents were barely able to make it past my sister's death, and it took them years to do so. Imagine what would happen if they lost another daughter to criminals. And imagine how much worse it'll be if they found out that I was putting myself in these kinds of situations willingly and had lied to them.

However, if I turn back now, how will I be able to look myself in the mirror? After coming all this way, I'd have quit right before the finish line. I'd never realize the good I could have done. But then again, for all I know, the only thing waiting on the other side of the finish line could be death.

Uncertainty surrounds me. The one thing I do know is that I can't turn back from whichever decision I make. If I choose to move forward on this path, I'll have crossed the point-of-no-return and will have chosen to go to death's door. I will have chosen to go into the shrouded abyss.

And I don't know where this abyss will end.

My knuckles turn white as I squeeze the steering wheel. I can barely even keep my mind on the road. My heart is low, and it feels like an unbearable weight crushes down on it. As I come to a stoplight, I stare at my reflection in the rear-view mirror. I look deep into the brown eyes that stare back at me. These eyes have done almost nothing but lie for the past few days. Lied to the punks I took down. Lied to my parents. And maybe, I've been lying to myself. Maybe Cap was right. Maybe they were right in the interview when they asked me why I was doing this.

Maybe it really is because she's gone.

I'm not sure where I'm going. I've been driving aimlessly since I left the bar-b-que. My gaze returns to the street light as it switches from red to green. I know where I have to go. It's the one place where I can never lie to myself. The one place where everything is clear—the one *person* who is always there for me: Angela.

* * *

She's always here. Here, under the shade of this ancient oak tree, I can always find her patiently waiting for me. Always the perfect listener, she never says a word back or interrupts me in any way.

But then again, that is what tombstones do.

Angela Rocha
January 7, 1964 to May 31, 1984
Loving Daughter and Sister

Every time I come here, it is the same. No matter the years that have passed, it seems too surreal to see her name on this weathered headstone. Maybe my mind still refuses to accept this fact, even fifteen years after her funeral. A part of me still thinks that she will come walking in through the front doors one day.

My heart sinks as I read the inscription. It feels as helpless as it did the night she was taken. I feel like the seven-year-old girl again who just learned that her sister would never come home.

And I die a little more each time.

***

The night Angela died was the night I learned what true helplessness is. My mom had put me to bed at seven just like she always did. But as usual, I was still awake when the clock struck nine. My brother was out on a camping trip with the Boy Scouts. All he ever talked about was how he was on track to become the youngest Eagle Scout in his troop. I remember thinking that Angela was out later than usual. On Tuesday night's Angela did some volunteer work at the local soup kitchen. In fact, three afternoons of her week were normally spent at some kind of charity.

But then the doorbell rang. My first thought was that Angela must've forgotten her keys. It wouldn't be the first time. Like always, I left my bed and came to the top of the stairs. I heard the door open, but I didn't hear mama's voice greet Angela or chastise her for being late. In fact, I didn't hear my mother say a word. I heard somebody step into the house. From my angle, I could not see the visitor's face, but I noticed his recognizable blue uniform. With a gun holstered around his belt, his golden badge remained pinned to his chest.

My first emotion was confusion. Why did this policeman stand where my sister should have been? Maybe a part of me knew. Maybe a part of me—a part deep inside—knew what was happening. Because without thinking, my fingers grasped the handrail.

"Mr. and Mrs. Rocha, I'm sorry to barge in like this."

"What is it, officer?"

"It's about your daughter…"

My hand instinctively tightened its grip around the railing.

The man could barely speak and he did not even look my parents in the eyes, knowing the pain his words would cause. "There's... there's been a shooting."

Standing on the top of the stairs, out of view from everyone else, I don't think I really understood what he was saying or was about to say. I didn't understand why my parents remained so silent or why the policeman acted so strangely.

"Your daughter... s—she was killed."

He said those words so quickly and softly that I barely heard them. And when I did realize what he had uttered, I thought that this was some kind of a dream. I could not comprehend the officer's words. I could not understand why my parents broke down into uncontrollable sobs. I could not understand why the officer did not try to console them and just stood there, helplessly watching.

Angela dead? What did that even mean? She couldn't have just left the house never to come back. That didn't happen in real life, did it? Any moment now, she'd walk back into the house. She had to. This is not how it happens. People don't just leave and never come back. Not without saying goodbye.

But as I stood there, listening to the weeping of my mother and bawling of my father, I could not move a muscle. My eyes stayed on the officer as he remained motionless. No matter how hard I tried, I could not go down there; nor could I go back to my room. And so I just stood at the top of the steps... helpless.

It was on those steps that reality began to set in. As my head replayed those solemn words over and over again, it finally began to understand. This was not a dream. There was no waking up from this. And Angela was not going to come home.

In those moments, my childhood ended. Innocence was replaced with harsh reality.

My heart suddenly began racing as my free hand formed into a tight fist. For the first time in my life, it felt as if a heavy weight dropped onto my heart, and I could not remove it no matter how hard I tried. At the center of the whirlwind stood one simple question: why Angela? Of all the people that could have died this night, why my big sister?

It was that night that I learned what loss feels like. I learned what it meant to be helpless. It's not the sudden rush of emotions. It's not the flood of grief. It's the slow reality that sets in. The reality that makes you realize how little you really are. The reality that nothing lasts forever. The reality that with each passing moment, we lose the ones we love.

And there is nothing we can do to stop it.

***

To this day, I have not found the answer to my question. But the one thing I have learned is that death is not considerate of anything. It has no bias.

I keep my gaze focused on Angela's headstone as I relive that fateful night. Staring at the tomb for the thousandth and first time, I finally do arrive at a realization. No matter how much I deny it, I still refuse to let Angela go—I still cannot accept what happened all those years ago.

And there is one more thing that I finally accept. The question that has haunted me—the question asked by my interviewers—I finally know the answer. The answer is most definitely 'yes'. It *is* because of Angela that I took this job. It *is* because of her that I have come this far.

Angela was simply a victim who was at the wrong place at the wrong time. One of the patrons of the kitchen had double-crossed a local drug lord, and a hit had been put out for him. Ten minutes before Angela's shift ended, a white van filled with four young men pulled up to the kitchen's glass doors. The van's doors opened, revealing four AK-47s aimed right at the building. And in the next moment, they lit the place up.

The ironic thing is that the man they'd come for did not die. He was in the bathroom when the drive-by occurred. Instead of hitting him, the bullets completely destroyed the building from the outside-in, wounding seventeen people in the process.

But one person was killed.

The worst part of it was when my parents learned that Angela did not die instantly. She was shot through her chest seven times. The bullets did not hit her heart or brain, which would have caused an instant death. Instead, they tore her chest to shreds. As she lay there helpless, blood filled her lungs and suffocated her. By the time the paramedics arrived, she was only moments away from death.

It was a slow death… a painful death.

A security camera caught the license plate of the shooters. Within the week, all four were arrested. One was over the age of eighteen and got the death penalty. The other three were minors and were treated as such in the courts. By now, all three of them will be out of prison.

I take a deep breath as I run my hand along the top of the tombstone. I know my parents and brother have found their peace. What happened to Angela occurred fifteen years ago and they have been able to come to terms with it through their faith.

But I can't.

No matter how long it's been, it remains fresh on my mind every day. I have searched through religion and have not been able to do what they did. I can't let this go. Maybe it is because I was so young. Maybe it is because Angela was everything to me.

Or maybe it is because I don't want peace.

I don't know what it is I'm looking for. I can't figure out what is holding me back. But I now know one thing for sure. Come Monday, I'll be back in my office. Cap said that I should take the week off to figure out if I really want to do this, but I know the answer to that. Visiting here has reaffirmed it.

With every punk I take off the streets, I save countless lives. I will beat down punks like Miller and put my life on the line every day if it means that a little girl will get to see her big sister one more time. I'll be smarter. Stronger. I'll do whatever I have to do to make it, even if I have to lie a million times. If I have to lose myself to my duty, then so be it. This is what I'll do to honor Angela's memory.

I owe it to myself.

CHAPTER 5
PARTNERS

Monday morning comes quickly. Bryan is not in his office and the door is closed, but unlocked. At first, I feel wrong for going into his office when he's not there, but then I remember that he did the same thing to me. I guess it's an eye for an eye.

I lightly close the door behind me before switching on the lights. As I do, I realize that this is my first time in his office. The setup is just as I imagined: simple and mostly unadorned. It's the same size as mine, except Bryan's has a window that lends a view of the parking lot. Or at least it would if the blinds weren't closed.

Mirroring my own office, there's a wooden desk decorated with a large computer monitor, several photos, a lamp, printer, and a can full of pencils and pens. His is more ordered than mine; all his files are neatly organized in the filing cabinet instead of being scattered across his desk. His framed certifications and awards hang from the wall behind his desk. There's also a bookshelf next to the plaques that is half-filled with books. They appear to be mainly novels. I wouldn't have imagined Bryan to be much of a reader.

I'm not exactly sure what Cap expected me to find in here. But remembering the way he said it, a part of me is a little apprehensive about finding out what he was referring to. Walking over to Bryan's desk, I look down at the photos. I do a double-take, not believing my eyes. Bryan is actually smiling. And it's not that awkward sort he did when we first met.

The first photo shows Bryan standing alongside another man on a fishing boat. I see Galveston Island in the distant backdrop. With the sun setting behind them, they're dressed in their fishing gear and proudly show their catches to the camera. Bryan holds a forty-pound tarpon and his friend has a similar-sized fish. They're both triumphantly lifting the fishes over their head, and their smiles say it all. Half of me can't believe that this is the same man who is my no-nonsense, machine-like partner. The satirical part of my mind is convinced that this has to be some kind of twin brother. Looking at the man next to Bryan, something about him just screams police officer.

My gaze travels onto the next photo. I know it's at the Houston Zoo from all the times I visited there growing up. The photo was taken from just outside the famous lion enclosure. A lion looks at the camera from behind the thick glass. Bryan wears a t-shirt and shorts, and a two-year-old boy sits on his shoulders. The boy is wearing an over-sized cap, his hands around Bryan's head. There's a beautiful blonde woman wrapped in one of Bryan's arms. Her slender figure is a perfect complement to Bryan's powerful frame. The smiles in this picture are nothing but joyful.

There are four more pictures lined up on the desk, and each of them either holds the woman and child or the other man from the fishing boat. But before I can really study any of them, I am no longer alone in the room.

I look up and see Bryan standing on the other side of the desk. His arms are crossed. "What are you doing?"

"Nothing. I was just looking for you."

"Normally when an office door is closed, it means that you shouldn't go in there."

"Sorry." My gaze focuses on his left hand. There is a small mark where the wedding ring would be. It's all starting to make sense.

His eyes follow mine. "Ana?"

Suddenly, I don't feel the same about him. "I wanted to talk to you about something, Bryan."

"What?"

"Seems I was wrong last Friday. I had no reason to be mad at you. It was my fault that we lost a suspect. You were right… and I apologize."

A part of me can't believe the words coming out of my mouth. And I don't think he can either. For a few long moments, he blankly stares at me before he finally musters a reply. "…it… you're not the one who should be apologizing, Ana. I was wrong to be that hard on you. Your life is more important than catching any punk. This job… I guess it makes you impassive sometimes. Sometimes we get too caught up in trying to catch the bad guys that we forget to watch the backs of the good ones." He takes a deep breath. "I'm sorry."

"No hard feelings." I hold out my hand. "It's a new week so let's just start fresh. Maybe we can actually get to know each other this time."

Bryan slightly smiles. And this time, it is a genuine smile—the same kind he had in the photos. He takes my hand and firmly shakes it. "Deal."

For a moment, I start to think that we've got a chance.

***

"So what do they call you, champ?"

I already know what his name is from his file, but I have to play the part. Seeing his expression, I think he's about to say it. However, his eyes suddenly show a change of heart as he gets second thoughts. "You gotta be a loyal customer before I give you that."

"And what's your definition of loyal?"

He thinks to himself, still wearing the same cautious expression that he's displayed since Bryan and I started speaking to him a few minutes ago. Probably wondering why this strange couple is being so friendly to him. But I bet deep in his heart he knows exactly why we're talking. "…three buys."

"So what do you want me and my boyfriend to call you until then?"

His gaze darts to Bryan and then comes back to me as if he's trying to figure out how we could be a couple. I wouldn't blame him for that. "Why'd you need to call me anything?"

"I wanna see if you got work?" I really am starting to feel like a drugee with all this lingo.

The target's eyes widen for a moment. Standing in the uncovered parking lot, Bryan and I are on the other side of the car from the man. To him, this is just a random conversation; however, it is anything but that. This morning we got a tip that this man—known on the streets as Damian—would be in this part of town. And after a rather long stakeout in my Avenger, we spotted him pulling into this parking lot only minutes ago.

Damian's dark skin is covered in sweat. His rough beard and hair are unkempt. His eyes, which would have been bloodshot a few hours earlier, still have remnants of the drugs he was taking this morning. On top of his skinny figure, he wears a dirty t-shirt that's two sizes too big and a pair of rugged shorts. There are two reasons people dress like this. One is because they think it's stylish. The second—and the more important reason—is because it's easy to pack heat under the loose clothing.

Even from here, I can smell the stench of his foul breath. And it tells me that he hasn't brushed his teeth in days. His dirty yellow Toyota Corolla is just as filthy as he is, outside of the expensive and polished rims decorating its wheels. Just like him, it smells like a skunk is in there.

The target finally replies. "…why you think I'm sellin' what you think I'm sellin'?"

Placing both hands on the hood of his dirty car I lean in a bit. "Look, I know you sellin' stones."

"How?"

I roll my eyes annoyingly. Please don't make me beg. "Because you drive a shitty-ass car that has ten grand rims like every other dealer I've bought from, and because your eyes bug'n and I can smell it all over you."

Damian is silent for several seconds. These mixed signals I'm sending are doing a number on his brain. "Ya'll ain't cops, right?"

"Do we look like cops?"

"I dunno. But you definitely don't look like a couple."

"We're new in town. Our neighbor sells, but he's a rip-off." Just as those words leave my mouth, I realize that I just put myself in a corner.

"Your neighbor?"

I nod. *Whatever you do, don't ask me his name.*

"What's his name?"

Think fast. "Can't tell you that until you're a loyal seller." *Good recovery there, Ana.*

"Loyal?"

I smirk as I playfully wink at him. "Sold three times to us."

After a long moment, the man slightly smiles. "...name's Damian."

Finally.

Bryan takes the reins of the conversation. "Oliver is our neighbor. So you sellin' stones or not?"

Damian scratches the top of his head with his long index finger. "I... it depends."

Bryan let out an annoyed sigh. "Look man, my girl and I are easy money for you. But if you ain't got the guts then—"

"Hey! I got the guts."

"Then we good?"

He takes a deep breath, knowing this is his last chance to turn away. But like all other dealers, he'll never say 'no' to an easy score. "...how much you want?"

"100 grams—how much will it be?"

He looks over at me and smirks. "For ya'll? Well, ya'll get the pretty girl discount."

***

The first thing I do as we pull out of the parking lot is jot down everything I need: name, physical description, license plate, and the place we're meeting Damian for the transaction tomorrow. And right after scribbling it all down, I blast the A/C on full in a vain attempt to counter this endless heat. It's hotter in the car than it was outside. Even at its maximum speed, the A/C is not working fast enough. This is something you never get used to no matter how long you've lived in Texas.

Not long after we're out-of-sight, Bryan speaks to me. His voice is back to normal and is as genuine as its been all day. "Looks like the tip was good. Good eye spotting him, Ana."

"Thanks."

"I've never heard of the 'pretty girl discount' before."

"Well, I doubt you get that kind of deal often."

He looks over at me with a small grin. "Well… there was that one time."

I lightly laugh. Was he actually trying to be funny? I could get used to this. "I don't think even a blind man would give it to you, Bryan."

Bryan's eyes go back onto the road. He leisurely grips the steering wheel with one hand as the other relaxes on the armrest. "You did good, Ana. Quick thinking—assertive—controlled the conversation and pulled on his strings."

"I have a pretty great partner backing me so of course I'd do well."

"Even still… but I can't believe he'd hit on you like that in front of your 'boyfriend'. But you saved the police force some money so I'm sure Cap will be proud of your charms. The only thing my charms have ever done is get the price raised."

I smile again before replying. "By the way, why'd you say our neighbor's name was Oliver?"

"I always use that name. Oliver Wayne if they want the full name. What name would you have used?"

"I actually don't know. Right when I mentioned the neighbor, I was afraid of what to say if he asked for a name."

"You played it well when he asked, but this is something to remember: no matter what name you say, it doesn't make a difference. When a dealer asks you who you're currently buying from, all they really want to see is if you're lying or not. If you can tell them with confidence and make them believe that you know what you're talking about and are what you say you are, they won't ask any more questions." Coming to a stop sign, the car rolls to a halt. He falls momentarily silent before looking at me. "How good of a liar are you, Ana?"

"I didn't practice it much growing up."

"But how good are you?"

I glance out the side window before turning back to my partner. I'm finally starting to feel the A/C's effects, but at this point, the conversation has me hardly thinking about it. "...seeing that I've been lying every day since I got this job and nobody has caught me yet—I'm afraid that I may actually be a natural."

"You'll be happy that you are." Bryan's eyes focus back on the road. He pushes onto the accelerator as we make a right turn to come onto the highway's ramp.

I slightly nod. "You want me to be there tomorrow?"

"Just in the vicinity in case things go south."

"Okay."

There is another silence as Bryan navigates onto the highway. It's still an hour before rush hour and we'll make it back to the station before the heavy traffic hits. "So you grew up in South Houston?"

"Close to Hobby," I reply. "Yourself?"

"Born in Cypress but grew up in Galveston. Which explains my love for fishing."

"Are you any good at fishing?'

"Well, I love it. But last time we went fishing, my six-year-old nephew caught more fish than I did, so I'm far from an expert."

I let out a light laugh. "I see. And what brought you into our *glamorous* profession?"

"Well, I originally wanted to play for the Houston Oilers?"

"What stopped you?"

"Two things." He looks at me with a smirk. "Talent and ability."

I smile back in amusement.

"But after that dream was killed, I decided I wanted to join the police force. My daddy was a policeman and so was his daddy. I guess it's a family trade." There is a pause. "But what makes a nice gal like you end up in a car with me?"

I look out the side window. "Family—but not in the way you're thinking."

"Then how?"

"I had something—someone taken from me. And... I guess doing this is the way that I can keep myself from losing them."

***

My heart is racing when the time for the deal arrives. I wasn't even this nervous on my first day when I had to get rid of that dreaded five-hundred dollars. Maybe it's because the naivety I entered this job with has all but shriveled away. Or maybe it's because last time I took part in an arranged deal, I nearly got killed.

But this time I'm not alone.

The weathered parking lot is completely empty. The cemented ground is cracked up, the painted lines hardly visible. The meeting spot is surrounded by trees and natural Texas vegetation. I'd imagine that there are plenty of raccoons and possums sleeping in the bushes and tall grass. It's only a quarter-mile off Beltway 8. However, it's out of view from anyone on that highway. I live only a few miles away but have never even seen this place. I imagine this is the perfect meeting spot for this kind of exchange.

My partner puts me in position in the shrubs right outside the lot's southern edge. After getting me situated, Bryan gives me a slight nod before turning away and heading to his spot. His gesture is so simple that I almost don't catch it. There're no valiant words like the hero of a movie says before charging into a life-threatening battle. This isn't a moment taken from the pages of *Braveheart*. It's such a simple gesture that—for an instant—the whole situation almost feels anti-climactic.

I stay crouched down amid the thick greenery. From here, I'm completely undetectable to the casual eye, but will be close enough to all the action. Dressed in a pair of rugged jeans and a dark top, my radio remains strapped to my waist and my gun is in hand.

We got here an hour before the scheduled time, but Bryan told me not to lollygag around as we prepared everything. Dealers usually show up very late for the first deal—normally as a show of power—but every once in a while they roll up way too early, typically if they're suspicious of the buyers.

And they never show up alone.

The sky is cloudless and the air is still while the sun mercilessly beats down on me. The endless humidity only makes it worse. I feel drenched in my own sweat. The one thing I forgot to bring was a water bottle, and the cynical part of my mind tries to convince me that I'll dehydrate before Damian ever even arrives.

No matter how long you live in Texas, you never get used to the heat. I guess it's the same way a soldier never really gets used to war. There's not a bird in the sky; the only thing here other than us are countless flies buzzing around.

Bryan certainly wasn't lying about them showing up late. It's an hour 'til noon—an hour past the meeting time—and there's still no sign of Damian. Bryan is patiently sitting in his running vehicle while I impatiently drown in my own sweat. I've lost count of the number of mosquitoes I've swatted by now. A part of me despises Bryan for being in the A/C while I'm dying out here. However, the other part of my mind is thankful that he's putting his life on the line more than I am.

But before I can grow too envious, Damian's yellow Corolla shows up. And as predicted, he's not alone. Damian shows up with two lackeys. Or as dealers say it—Damian is rolling three deep. God, I've got to stop thinking in all this dealer lingo.

The car stops a few yards away from Bryan's vehicle before both parties step out almost simultaneously. Even from here, I can feel my partner's confidence and can see it in his step. He possesses this aura that seems to suddenly appear when he is in his alter ego. The grip around my Glock tightens even though I don't have a clear shot from this position. But if things start to go south, Bryan will signal me by looking to his right. I'll only have to dart a few yards to get off a shot. And I can easily do that before any of those punks know what's coming.

The air is tense. Even more so because I can't hear what they're saying. From their body language, it seems that they don't suspect a thing. But Damian and his crew are not being overly friendly either. Bryan has the money in a brown paper bag and the dealers have the stones—I mean drugs—in a similar bag. Everyone's expressions remain straight, not giving anything away. But I suddenly see Bryan slightly smile as he says something. And after a long, awkward moment, all three thugs break into friendly laughter.

Moments later, the exchange is made. Bryan's charms stop Damian from even bothering to count the money. As quickly as the deal began, it ends. Within five minutes of pulling onto the lot, Damian shakes Bryan's hands and leaves.

And by next week's end, Damian will be locked up.

***

The week goes by faster than any I've ever experienced, drawing to an end in the blink of an eye. By the time Friday rolls around, Bryan and I have completed three successful deals with two more set up for the coming week. Apparently, racking up two successful exchanges in a week is considered a 'good' week, and we blew past that counting the deals we've set up for the following week. We use each deal as an opportunity to tag the dealers and figure out where they're staying. Within a week to two weeks of each exchange, the dealers will be busted and brought in. By then, they'll have sold to plenty of other clients and won't even be thinking of us as the ones who busted them. The drugs we buy off of them, along with anything that's on them when they're arrested, will be the primary evidence used to lock them up.

Bryan says it's been some of the most productive days he's ever witnessed, and Cap is more than pleased with how we're working together now. The only downside to all the deals can be summed up in one word: paperwork. Lots and lots of paperwork—nearly eight hours for each case to be exact. But knowing the difference we make with each deal and bust is worth it. Each dealer we put away is one less criminal out on the streets. And if it means that we've saved even one life down the road, then it's worth it.

I find myself in the break room an hour before quitting time on Friday. As I sit at one of the tables, Bryan stands above me and looks at the crowd of people listening to his tale. For all his attributes, I never imagined him to be a captivating storyteller. Maybe it's a trait he's picked up after reading all those novels on his bookshelf. Seems I learn more and more about him every day.

Maybe a time will come when I can actually call him a friend.

"So the dealer tries to raise the price on us right before the buy," Bryan tells the other officers. "I'm about to try and negotiate it back down all nicely—but Ana had other ideas."

The small crowd hinges on his every word.

"Before I can do anything, Ana stares the dealer in the eyes and—without blinking—she shows the dude that she's packing a gun." Bryan lightly lifts the tail ends of the shirt to demonstrate what I did. "And with all the conviction in the word, she says 'Keep talking like that and I'll put so many bullet holes in your body that you won't know which ones to breathe from and which ones to shit from'."

"Holy crap," one of the officers utters.

Bryan looks in that man's direction. "And do you know what the dude does? After nearly wetting his pants, he almost gives us the drugs for *free!*"

The audience bursts into laughter.

I feel a couple of pats on the back, but keep my gaze on my partner's face. Bryan laughs along with the rest of the crowd. I can hardly imagine that a week ago I thought I hated the man. It's amazing what difference a few days can make. Feeling my gaze, he glances down at me and shoots me a friendly wink.

However, there is one man in the break room not enjoying the story: Mark Davidson. In fact, as I catch him leaning against the far wall, his expression is the opposite of everyone else's. The more people laugh, the more disgusted his face grows. When the laughter begins to die out, he starts to gradually make his way toward the crowd, eyes on Bryan.

Mark loudly speaks above the laughter, putting out its remnants. "That's real cute."

Everyone turns to look at him.

"You know what happens to rookies that do good? Well, we've all seen it." Mark looks directly at me as he arrives at the edge of the crowd. It parts like the Red Sea for him. "They all have the biggest sophomore slumps."

"Davidson, I'm trying to remember," Bryan sarcastically begins, "When's the last time you did this good in a week? Because my mind is not remembering a time when that happened."

Mark silently glares at my partner but steps forward until he's only a few feet from Bryan's intimidating figure. Mark is a big guy, but he's not as well-built as Bryan, so he has to look up into Bryan's eyes to meet his stare.

"And when you add up all that Ana's done since she's got here, that's *exactly* what she's done," Bryan continues. "Not that I'm keeping count or anything, but it seems like you're the one in the slump here."

There's a tense moment—too long of a moment for my personal liking. For a second, I think that there is going to be a brawl in the break room. I can see the idea being considered in Mark's eyes. The news headline flashes through my mind: *Two Officers Taken to Hospital after Fistfight at Police Station.*

Oh, God. Please don't happen.

Mark finally glances down at me again and then back at Bryan. He takes a small step closer. "Riding high, aren't we Bryan? Well, let's not so easily forget the past."

The smile on Bryan's face suddenly disappears. His hand clenches into a tight fist. For a moment, I think Mark is a dead man. "Don't start something you can't end, Mark."

After a long moment, Mark turns away and my fears disperse. "I'm not starting anything. Just reminding us all that sometimes the past repeats itself." He slightly turns his head toward me. "And I'd hate for a pretty gal like her to be on the six o'clock news for all the wrong reasons."

CHAPTER 6
TWO LIVES

"The Bible tells us much."

Like every Sunday for as long as I can remember, I find myself sitting in church. I hardly even recollect a time where I've actually missed a service. More than that, I've been coming to the exact same church since I could first walk. But like many Sundays I've experienced, today is one day that I would rather have skipped.

I sit on the edge of the pew underneath the high ceiling. Mama is right next to me, the rest of the family nearly lining up the entire bench. We're all dressed in our Sunday Bests, but we're not in the front row like usual. That's my fault since I kept the rest of the family waiting. Even though both her kids have moved out, my mother still insists on us all riding here together.

"God separates right from wrong—truth from lies—light from dark."

Mirroring most Catholic priests, ours is dressed in his seasonal robes as he stands at the altar. With his wrinkly skin, he looks like a Hispanic Emperor Palpatine. All he's missing is the hood. A cross hangs from his neck while an open and marked Bible rests on the podium in front of him. Behind him is a window painting depicting the Virgin Mary as she holds her new-born baby. Several more glass murals line up the grand hall's walls as they portray images of Jesus' life.

"And one of the evils God warns us about is the evil of lying."

I keep my gaze glued to the red carpet. I can't even look at the priest today. Every time I do, I feel my stomach turn on itself. I initially felt this uneasiness on the first Sunday after I became a narcotics officer. It's now been three Sundays since I started that path and this feeling grows worse and worse with every passing service. Today, I feel like puking my guts out.

Is this how hypocrites feel?

The church is at its maximum capacity. Every bench has one too many people on it, leaving some of the attendants forced to stand along the back wall. Two sets of circular pillars stand parallel to one another, going from the front of the church's hall to the back. The domed ceiling amplifies the priest's voice. And the more I hear his words, the sicker I become. Of all the topics he could have picked, why this one? I finally bring myself to look up at him. Standing tall and proud, Emperor Palpatine's gaze goes over the faces of each and every one of his disciples.

"Lying is the source of all evils. It is the sin that leads to and increases others. It is the sin that removes people from Heaven and puts them in Hell."

My heart begins beating faster as I start to sweat. I don't know why this is happening to me. It's not like he's talking to only me. It's just a speech. I take a deep breath, trying to calm myself down... but it is to no avail.

"It's the sin that creates wicked people."

C'mon. Change the subject already.

"It knocks even the most righteous people off from their pedestals and brings them down into the valley of darkness."

The priest's gaze arrives on me. And it stops. For a long moment, there is silence. His eyes are locked with mine as if he is staring into my very soul. It's almost like he is speaking directly to me. As if he knows everything I have been doing. As if he knows of all the sins I've committed on this road I'm traveling.

The dam bursts. Guilt pours out of my heart, flooding through my body. It goes to every corner and into every crevice.

"It is the sin that takes one out of the favor of God."

I can't take this.

Without warning, I suddenly shoot up. I feel numerous gazes focus on me—including my own family's—but I ignore them. The priest pauses for a moment upon seeing me rise but then quickly continues his sermon. I don't hesitate as I hastily make my way toward the exit opposite of the stage. His voice trails behind me as he continues his speech against lying. But I block it all out. Amidst the stares and whispers, I push the heavy doors and leave the church behind me.

Minutes later, I find myself leaning against the church's exterior as my eyes look up at the heavens. There are only a handful of clouds visible in the blue skies. The sun is scorching and mercilessly beats down on me, but I don't give it a second thought right now. Compared to how hot I was getting inside there, this feels like winter.

The guilt that drowned my soul is still there. Since I've started working, all I've seemingly done is lie. Lie to the crooks I try and bring down. Lie to my brother. My father. And—worst of all—my mother.

When I stood before Angela's tombstone, I made a promise to do whatever it took to carry out my duty of cleaning up the streets. But coming to places like this and hearing Emperor Palpatine's lecturing reminds me about where my choices may be taking me. And the thought of where I may find myself at the end of all this keeps sleep far away from me on some nights.

"Ana?"

I tear my gaze away from the sky and see my mother coming toward me, a worried expression spread across her face. She embraces me into a protective hug.

"Are you feeling okay, sweetie?"

"I'm fine, mom." Here I go again with the lying. "Just got a little queasy inside there."

She puts her hand on my forehead. "You do seem a little warm, Ana. Maybe you ate something."

"I think I'm just tired."

"You've been so distant today. Is there something bothering you?"

She's not exaggerating. Ever since I received my badge and gun, I've been distant from my family. And the gap only grows with each passing day. I don't know why. I try to keep my two lives separate. But the harder I try, the more it seems that my life as Officer Rocha is beginning to creep into my life as Ana. It's as if everything I believed to be true is changing.

What used to be sin has become duty.

But what can I tell my mother? What can I tell the woman who raised me? The truth will only break her heart. It's far too late to come clean now. I have become the boy who swallowed the fly. And now, all I can do to cover up my first lie is to utter an even bigger one.

The scary thing is that I am a great liar.

***

I'm filling out paperwork when Bryan enters my office. He carries a white bag in one hand and lightly closes the door behind him. His face is never overly jovial, but there is a hint of warmth in it today. It's the same kind of warmth a veteran athlete would show their protégée on the team. I might even call it friendliness. He casually begins to make his way over to my desk. "You worked through your lunch break, Ana."

"Really?" I look up at the clock. Sure enough, it's just striking one in the afternoon.

"That paperwork must be mighty interesting."

I would love to say that the paperwork was so exciting that it made me lose track of time. But truthfully, it was the memory of the minister's words that caused my thoughts to stray.

"I brought you lunch." Bryan slightly raises up the bag, showing me the sandwich shop's logo. I recognize the restaurant as the one from just around the corner.

"My hero."

He sets the bag on the tabletop. "Hope you like turkey sandwiches."

"Who doesn't?"

"Vegans… or at least I'd think."

Was that another joke? I'm starting to like my partner more every day. Rummaging through the bag, I pull out a thick and cold sandwich enclosed in Saran Wrap. Trapped between the top and bottom of a sub are several slices of freshly cut turkey, along with lettuce, tomatoes, and pickles. After the sandwich, I pull out a water bottle along with a few condiments.

"You thought of everything, didn't you?" I remark.

He takes a seat across from me. "It's what partners do."

I smile before starting to unwrap the sandwich. To think that not too long ago I hated this man's guts and now he's buying me food. Who could've predicted this?

Bryan's eyes glance over my desk. He hardly ever comes in here. And when he does, it's only ever for a quick moment. But today, he's not in a rush and neither am I. His gaze travels over the pictures on my desk: me with my parents, me with Ramon and Laura, and me with Angela.

He reaches over and picks up the last photo as I bite down on my lunch. Everything is fresh: the turkey, vegetables, and the bread. I can taste the quality of it all. The turkey is juicy and seasoned with plenty of spices to give it flavor. The tomatoes and lettuce taste like they were grown and plucked out of the ground today. The pickles have the perfect tang: sour but not overly bitter. And the bread is soft, almost melting in my mouth.

But as I enjoy the free meal, I watch his expression. I know what's in the picture. It was taken when I was four-years-old. Angela took me to Herman Park on a Saturday afternoon. I remember the day clearly. Usually, Herman Park is packed on the weekends since its right outside the zoo. But this day, for one reason or another, it seemed like we had the place to ourselves. Angela was never much of a cook, and I doubt our picnic would have received a five-star review, but all I can remember from that day is the laughter.

In the photo, we're both facing the camera with the lake in the background. My hair is tied back into a ponytail, a large bow on top, while her beautiful locks are let down. I'm sitting on her shoulders with my elbows resting on top of her head.

"Is this your sister?"

I nod. "D you have any siblings?"

Bryan smiles at me. "Three older brothers."

"Holy crap." My eyes slightly widen. "They must've made your life hell."

"Oh, trust me. They did… until I got bigger than them. Today, they are almost too terrified to speak to me," he jokes.

I lightly smirk.

He glances back down at the photo. "But it seems like you two are close."

"*Were* close."

Bryan's gaze suddenly breaks away from the picture, returning back to me. From one look, he knows exactly what I mean. His expression slowly changes, and I see compassion in his eyes. "…I'm sorry."

"It's alright." I pause for a moment. "She was more than a sister, really. She was my second mom, best friend, and everything that I wanted to be when I grew up. Angela always looked out for me… and always loved me."

"I don't doubt it." He focuses on the image once again. "You can see it in her eyes."

"See what?"

"Her love for you." Bryan sets the photo down. "I'm sure she'd be proud."

***

The street is littered with corpses. They're shot up, lying on the road like sacks of meat. Buildings are ablaze as deadly flames consume vehicles. Black, suffocating smoke blocks out the heavens. But continuous gunfire drowns out the flames. The gunfire is endless, coming from every direction.

I'm paralyzed as I stand in the middle of it all. My gaze stays focused on the corpse resting at my feet, unable to fathom whose dead body I'm staring at.

It's me.

On its back, the corpse's dead eyes stare up at the dark heavens. The body is pale... lifeless. One bullet hole is in its head. The other is in its heart.

Next to my dead body are the corpses of my family. Mother. Father. Ramon. Laura. Feeling something, I raise my gaze and see a faceless gunman standing before me. The barrel of his pistol aims straight at my eyes. Unable to move, unable to do anything, I watch as he slowly pulls the trigger to end my life.

I suddenly wake with a start. Shooting upright on my bed, I instinctively grab a handful of my blanket and clench it close to my chin. My gaze wildly darts around the dark room. I'm drenched in my own sweat. My breathing is quick—heartbeats even faster.

Why does this keep happening to me?

Closing my eyes, I focus like I was trained to do in Taekwondo. My hand gradually lets go of the covers, allowing it to fall onto my lap. It takes a few minutes, but I soon have my breathing under control. And within moments, my heart rate is no longer running wild.

This is not the first nightmare I've experienced. They started almost a week and a half after I received my badge. But they've been getting worse and more detailed with each passing vision. And this time, it felt too real.

Surrounded by the night's pitch blackness, I sit there for a few minutes. But I soon swing by legs over the edge. I slowly get out of bed and make my way to the opposite bedroom.

What does this all mean? Is it a warning? A premonition? Or is it simply a manifestation of all my fears? Only God knows the answer to that.

Arriving in the next bedroom that holds the web of facts, I switch on the lights. Without thinking, I slump down against the wall opposite of the web and stare at Angela's picture. Tonight, her smile makes me a little sick, and I don't know why. I feel anger swell up inside me the more I look at it... but I can't tear my eyes away.

After what feels like a long time, my gaze gradually travels from her picture and onto everything else. Sleep is far from me as I begin to read everything that is taped to the wall. There are a few observations, some evidence too, but the wall is mostly covered in questions.

Which gang did the shooters belong to?
Why did they choose the kitchen as their attack point?
Who ordered the hit?

I don't know if I will ever discover the answer to any of my questions. But what I know most is that the hope of one day coming face-to-face with the one responsible for ordering the hit that took my sister's life is what drives me. It is what makes me willing to endure a thousand nightmares.

It's what makes me strong enough to handle whatever this duty throws at me.

***

After the nightmare, I don't sleep a wink. I stay slumped against the bedroom wall, keeping my gaze focused on the sister I would give anything to hold one last time.

It's not even half past five in the morning when my home phone rings. My heart skips a beat when the phone's shrieking ring abruptly breaks the apartment's silence, throwing me out of my trance. I quickly stumble to my feet. Quickly rushing out of Angela's memorial room, I grab the phone by its third ring and answer it by the fourth.

"Hello?"

"Ana. It's me."

"What's going on Bryan?" What's Bryan doing calling me this early? It's the first time he's ever called me at my apartment. He usually just pages me. It takes me a moment to realize I haven't fallen asleep and am not dreaming this. Something must be up.

"How quickly can you get to the station?"

"How quickly do you need me?"

"Ten minutes ago."

"I'm leaving right away."

***

Dawn is breaking when I arrive at the station. The whole way here, I weaved through the early morning rush like James Bond, thinking of the thousand scenarios that Bryan could be calling me about. Each situation that played out in my head was deadlier than the last. Did he get a tip on a dealer? Are we raiding a stash house? Did some wanted criminal suddenly show up on the radar? The possibilities are endless.

I quickly make my way across the mostly empty parking lot and push through the station's doors. A rush of cold air hits me as I do. Bryan's waiting for me in the lobby next to the receptionist's desk. The secretary is away from her station, leaving just the two of us. His eyes are staring down at his watch when I enter the building, but his gaze immediately comes to me when he hears me arrive. This must be something urgent for him to be so anxious like this. Just one look at his demeanor and I can tell that something big is afoot.

"You look a bit flustered, Bryan."

He skips the pleasantries. With the state he's in, it's no surprise that he does. "You brought your gun and badge?"

"Always." I flash him my Glock and credentials.

"I got a call from an informant—Obadiah Holmes."

I've never heard of that one.

"He contacted me an hour ago, saying he saw a man we've been looking for near the Houston office of the Daniels Foundation. Holmes tailed the target back to a stash house that Holmes claims is operated by the dealer."

"Brave informant."

"He has his moments. Dealer's name is Raheem Moore."

"Name sounds familiar."

"It should. Moore works for the largest cartel in Houston. He's a slippery one though. But if the information Holmes gave me is correct, it could lead to a big bust. A good estimate is that there'll be four other dealers in a stash house run by Moore with 9 to 10 kilos of goods."

"How reliable is this Holmes guy?"

"That's the thing. He's been wrong before—enough times that his word won't be enough for Cap to mobilize SWAT or request a warrant." Bryan pauses for a moment. "He's not even an official informant anymore—he lost that status after his last bit of info made the department waste a lot of time and resources, leading to the suspect escaping. He's just an old contact of mine now."

"That's why you need more than his word."

Bryan simply nods.

"So what's the plan?"

"You and me will check out the place from afar to see if we can spot anything suspicious. Best case scenario, we see Moore himself."

"And the worst case scenario?"

Bryan slightly smiles. "We get shot."

"Yeah... let's avoid that one."

"That'd be a good idea. We want to at least get some sort of probable cause that the place is a stash house—enough evidence to justify a warrant and raid. If my man's story checks out, we can have a warrant within hours, and the stash house will be raided before sunset. Moore won't have a chance to escape this time."

CHAPTER 7
RECONNAISSANCE

It's unreal to see these hallways nearly deserted. It's only an hour before I usually arrive, but with only a skeleton crew at the station, it feels like I'm walking through a ghost town. The two of us quickly go down the empty corridor and into Bryan's office. There are two messenger bags on his desk: one green and the other black. He grabs the green one and hands it to me. It's not as light as it looks. Must be packing something serious.

As I open the top flap and stare into the bag's contents, Bryan closes the door before breaking the silence. "That's your field kit."

I rummage through the bag. A half-filled notebook, water bottle, books, and used pencil bag are the first things I see. Nothing out of the ordinary there. As for the bag, it's pretty worn down, missing a couple of buttons with several loose threads hanging off its sides. But when I dig a little deeper, I find a radio and high powered camera at the bottom. And beneath them is an extra clip for my Glock. Now I know what's making the bag heavy.

"Hopefully all you need to use is the camera. But there should be enough in there for you to maintain your cover if needed."

I look back at him and sling the bag's strap across my shoulder. "Here's hoping."

"Have you ever been to Third Ward?"

"Nothing more than seeing it from the highway. But I've heard enough about it."

Bryan slightly smiles. "Today's your lucky day then. You'll be seeing it firsthand."

Third Ward holds the highest homicide rate in Houston. In fact, it boasts the highest crime rate, period. It's been that way for as long as I can remember. All it's known for is gangs and crime. One look into the area and you get the sense that it's not the kind of place you want to be walking through alone. Especially at night. It's a sad story since Third Ward is one of the city's historically richest places.

"I guess there's a first time for everything," I quietly whisper. "Does Cap know about this op?"

Bryan lightly shrugs. "It's not strictly official. One thing you'll come to learn is that Cap prefers a 'don't ask, don't tell' philosophy when it comes to this sort of stuff."

"I see."

He grabs a folder off of his desk and takes a photo out of it before handing the picture to me. It's a mug shot. "Take a good look, Ana. It's a four-year-old picture, but should be good enough to recognize Moore by if you see him. He was picked up on charges of illegal possession of guns when this was taken. But the arresting officer didn't document the evidence properly, and Moore was let go on a technicality."

A dark-skinned man stares back at me from the photo. He has a rough, unkempt face and a buzz cut hairdo. Some sort of symbol is tattooed on the right side of his neck. It looks like a wave of fire. Moore's eyes hold the look of a devil. The structure of his head and neck give the impression that he possesses a lean body. He may not have the most intimidating figure, but his face appears violent enough. He'd be a handful in a fistfight.

"A year later, Moore shot down a cop before gunning down two civilians—a man and woman. The wife was three months pregnant. He did it when he was pulled over for breaking a signal. Probably had something on him that he didn't want the cop to find. The cop was a friend of this station's: Zhen Hue. He left behind a wife he had married a few months before." Bryan takes a long pause. In his eyes, I can see him reliving the nightmare. "Nobody cared… nobody except us."

I pick up the emotion is Bryan's voice as he utters those words. My gaze focuses back on the photo for a moment before returning to my partner. His eyes are filled with sorrow as silence engulfs the room.

Bryan takes a deep breath, his voice returning back to normal. "Moore disappeared and only popped up on the grid a couple of times afterwards, but we could never get official eyes on him."

I look back down at the killer.

"Memorize the face?" Bryan asks.

Handing the photo back to Bryan, I slightly nod. "It's not one that I'd forget easily."

"And hopefully it's one that we see today."

***

For the first time since I've met him, Bryan doesn't have a talk show or country music playing in the car. Instead, there is silence. Absolute silence. We are both lost in our own thoughts as we speed toward our destination.

Since taking the exit off of Highway 59 and entering Third Ward, I notice that the buildings continue to deteriorate the deeper we go into the area. This place always seemed a little worn down from the outside. But looking at it from within makes it become all the more real.

Beaten-down fences are topped with barbed wire, intimidating and loud dogs roam backyards as they bark at anything in sight, and windows are backed up by steel bars to keep intruders out. Those are the first things I notice. There aren't any new cars parked on the sides of the road and the ones that are don't look very inviting. As can be imagined, nobody is keeping up with trimming the hedges, cutting the grass, or keeping the walkways intact. Every building is run down and seems to have been built ages ago. There isn't a whole lot of upkeep here. I guess nobody here would want their house or shop looking too good. That'd probably just be an invitation for robbery.

Everyone we pass seems to be giving us an odd look, as if they know we don't belong. Our vehicle fits in, but maybe they can just sense that we're not from around here. They're dressed like you would expect people to be dressed in a poverty-stricken area like this. I don't observe a whole lot of people out. But at seemingly every corner, there are a couple of punk-looking guys hanging around. I'm sure they're up to more than just enjoying the hell-like heat.

My partner is unfazed and keeps his attention on the road. I wonder how many times he's been here before. Hopefully enough to know what he's doing. Just looking out at these mean streets is enough to give me the creeps. The thought that I'll soon be on them makes my stomach knot.

As we pass a blue bricked building made up of five double-story townhouses, Bryan breaks the silence but doesn't slow the car down. "This is it."

"Which building?"

"Far right."

I look at it as we drive by. The building is in no better or worse shape than any of the others. The window blinds are open, but the curtains are all pulled back while the glass is reinforced by steel bars, even the ones on the second floor. The front lawn is a mess of overgrown grass and weeds, and the weathered rooftop is in need of repair. The blue paint appears worn down. It seems that the building was painted navy blue when originally built. But now, it has been reduced to a powder blue. Three cars are parked outside its front door: a red Lexus, a black Toyota Camry, and a black Cadillac. The Lexus is in good condition and seems relatively new—it's probably the best car I've seen since coming here—but the other two look seven to eight-years-old. From our angle, none of the townhome's inhabitants are visible.

Bryan doesn't slow down. Instead, he makes a turn and the townhouse disappears out-of-sight behind another apartment complex. The vehicle gradually begins to arrive at a halt until it stops right outside a beaten-down and empty park's entrance. Switching the car into its parking gear before shutting it down, Bryan turns toward me. "You all set?"

Making sure that nobody is nearby, I quickly whip out my Glock. Bryan watches as I pull out its clip and check to make sure the weapon isn't jammed before loading and concealing it once again. I feel my heart slowly start to increase its pace. Is this all really happening? "Hopefully I don't need to use this."

"That would be ideal."

"So what's the plan?" I ask.

"I'll stakeout on the front side of the building. You swing around to the back. Go around the park and you should end up facing the back of the complex. We'll stake out for one hour tops—unless we get enough intel before."

"What are we looking for?"

"Any signs of criminal activity or Moore himself."

"Got it."

"Find a nice hidey-hole. Somewhere not too conspicuous and somewhere you won't be seen—especially from people inside the building. No matter what, don't cause a scene and don't step foot on their property. We don't have a warrant here. Strictly reconnaissance. Even if you see Moore and have a chance to take him down, do not engage unless you're being threatened. We don't want him; we want him, his crew, and whatever he might know."

I nod.

"Remember Ana, we're not in Sugarland or Clear Lake. This is Third Ward. This is the worst place to do any sort of op. Countless officers have been gunned down here. Treat every person with suspicions. Anybody suspicious comes near you, don't lower your guard. You don't know who is a lookout, and it's usually the person you least expect. Avoid as many people as you can. Whenever you're in doubt, err on the side of caution. As important as Moore is, your safety comes first. I won't be far if you need me."

"I can handle myself." I don't think I sound as confident as I intended to.

"Alright." Bryan gives me a quick nod. "Complete radio silence unless there's an audible."

"Will do. And Bryan?" I slightly smile at my partner. "Don't worry. We'll nail this son of a gun today."

With those words and without a second thought, I grab my messenger bag and exit the vehicle. As soon as I do, Bryan starts up the car and quickly departs, leaving me alone.

***

Here we go.

Slinging my messenger bag over my shoulder, I feel my gun strapped around my waist and underneath my shirt. The morning sun beats down on me and a few beads of sweat run down the back of my neck as I begin to make my way around the rusty-fenced park. All but one swing is broken, and the slides look like they were built during the Civil War. There's not a soul anywhere near here. I doubt many kids would even want to play in a place like this, even if it is their only option.

I never thought that I'd end up here: walking alone through the most crime-ridden part of Houston with nothing but a pistol and my wits to defend myself. The countless negative outcomes possible run through my mind. And the more they do, the more my stomach turns over on itself. It makes me feel sick. A part of me doesn't believe this is happening. It wants to believe that I'll wake up from this dream at any moment. But my instincts know better.

There's nobody in sight and no other sound except for my footsteps and a few bugs in the grass. The stillness only makes me more nervous. Walking down the cracked pavement, one hand holds onto my bag's strap while the other stays by my side, close to my gun.

My hair is tied back into a long ponytail. Dressed in a pair of blue jean shorts that go to my knees and a brown, short-sleeved top, I blend right in with the locals. The clothes aren't anywhere near posh, and there's nothing to tell me apart from anyone I might come across. But even so, I feel out-of-place. Everyone here will see right through me. I don't belong here. I know it. And I fear that they'll know it too.

A couple of women come walking down the sidewalk across the street from me. I almost jump when I notice them, but somehow keep my composure. *Calm down, Ana.* Damn, I'm so jittery right now—too on edge. The women are lowly talking to one another, but I hear remnants of their whispers. Dressed in shorts a bit too small and skimpy tank tops, they both shoot me a quick glance when they notice me before resuming their conversation. I don't look their way, not directly at least. However, I keep tabs on them from the corner of my eye. Not slowing down, I act like I'm not paying them any heed. The closer I get to them, the more my internal alarm starts to go off, wanting my hand to be as close to my gun as possible. I ignore it, acting natural.

The whole time, I envision the two of them suddenly drawing out their hidden weapons and gunning me down, killing me on the spot. What would Bryan think, having his partner killed within the first minute of the mission?

But they pass by harmlessly.

I breathe a sigh of relief. Those women are probably just out for a morning walk, but my mind is making everything a threat right now. As soon as they turn a corner and disappear, something else leaps into my path. It climbs and soars over a low fence, landing a few feet in front of me: a dog—a stray dog from the looks of it. It's big and looks like it can bite my head off in one swipe. It immediately whips its head toward me.

It growls, showing its teeth and hunter-like eyes. Oh, crap. My hand slowly inches toward my gun. My heart rate suddenly goes through the roof. "Get out of here."

The dog turns to fully face me, still growling.

My fingers graze my Glock's grip. There's no safety on it. If the dog makes a move, all I have to do is point and shoot. But it's close. Too close. If it jumps, I may not have time to take it down. And firing off a shot could blow this whole op. My breathing slightly quickens as my heart pounds against my chest. "Get out of here. Now."

Without thinking, I take a step forward and keep my gaze locked with the dog's. Suddenly, the beast turns around and takes off in the opposite direction. I breathe a sigh of relief and pull my hand away from my gun. Not even three minutes in and I'm already having a heart attack.

I take a few long breaths, calming myself down the best I can. *Come on, Ana. This is a walk in the park. You're just walking down the street. No big deal.*

After taking another look to make sure nobody's watching me, I continue down the path. Almost at the corner of the run-down street, I keep moving forward. I arrive at an intersection and turn the corner. My nerves are still a mess, but at least my breathing and heart have calmed down a bit—enough so that I can think straight. This sidewalk will lead me to the back of the complex. Hopefully there's a park or some trees that I could use as a lookout point.

Are those footsteps? I swiftly twirl around. My hand comes onto my pistol, but I don't draw it out. However, I find nothing behind me except for an empty pathway. My eyes scan the scene ten times over but see nobody. I swear I heard something. Maybe it's just my nerves. I take a deep breath to regain my senses before continuing down the sidewalk.

There's nothing heard except the echo of my own steps. I feel like there are eyes on me, but I don't know if I can even differentiate between my nerves and instincts as I turn another corner.

I stop.

Down the sidewalk is a group of three men. They're a rough-looking bunch, dressed in worn-down, loose shorts and shirts. The three of them are dressed in solid red, including their over-sized caps and shoes.

Oh, God. They haven't seen me yet. But I have to pass them if I stay on this road. I could keep moving down my original path and try to swing around from a longer route. But that'd burn more time, and I only have an hour. However, walking by them would be dangerous. There isn't another person on sight. I doubt they're just hanging out here to make small talk.

My stomach ties itself into a tighter knot. I take a deep breath as I keep my eyes on the pack. One of them, the leader from the looks of it, leans against a fence, while the other two listen to him speak. Under their baggy clothing could be anything from a knife to a gun. They give off the same foul vibe as Miller and his crew. For all I know, they could be murderers like he was. This could become the same disaster as before. I could end up blowing this whole op right here. Or even worse, I could get... I should turn away. My mind is screaming that.

...no. This job isn't about playing it safe. There's only one thing to do.

Eyes straight ahead, I start moving toward them. My heart starts beating faster.

Ba-dum... ba-dum... ba-dum.

It feels like it'll burst out of my chest at any moment, and the gut-wrenching knot in my stomach only makes it worse.

Ba-dum... ba-dum... ba-dum.

Somehow, I'm able to control my breathing and sweating. I barely maintain the confidence in my eyes. *Whatever happens, Ana, don't show any fear.* Keep it all inside. It'll only increase the chances of this all ending badly.

Ba-dum... ba-dum... ba-dum!

A few steps in, their leader notices me. He says something to the other two with a smile, and they both also turn toward me. Now they're exchanging glances with one another. I see the wicked smirks on their smug faces.

There's no backing out now, Ana.

The leader is no longer leaning against the fence. They're watching me as I near them, watching with the eyes of hyenas. They're all taller and seem stronger than me. They think that I'll be powerless against them—I can see it in their gazes. My heart pounds faster and faster with each step.

Ba-dum—ba-dum—ba-dum!

My mind screams for me to turn back around, thinking that there is no good outcome from this. *Keep yourself together, Ana.* With each step, I feel like I'm walking further and further into a den full of rabid animals that are waiting to pounce on a prey.

But today, I'm not going to be anyone's prey. I maintain my composure, at least on the outside. *Don't show any hesitation, Ana. And definitely don't show any fear.* Right now, you own these streets. Perception is reality, and you belong here. You have no reason to be afraid of them, but they have every reason to be afraid of you. Walk like these streets are yours and act like they're yours, and these punks won't dare do a damn thing.

I'm not even ten steps away from them. They break formation and step toward me as one of them speaks. "Where ya goin'?"

"You lost, girl? Ain't ever seen you 'round here," the leader snickers as he runs his hand through his dirty hair. "You look like you could use a friend."

I respond coldly, gaze locked with the punk's. "Beat it or you'll all have another thing comin'."

They don't. The leader stands in front of me and his boys fan out, trapping me in a semi-circle. "Don' be like that. We jus' wanna give you a *nice*, warm welcome."

I stare at his vile face dead in his eyes. Without missing a beat, I lift the tails of my shirt a bit, revealing the gun strapped around my waist. "Back off before I paint these streets with your guts."

Seeing my gun, the leader instinctively steps back and slightly raises his hands. His lackeys follow suit. By his reaction, I know none of them are carrying anything more dangerous than a pocketknife. "Alright, alrigh'. No need for any mess. We jus' wanted to welcome you to the neighborhood."

"Some welcome."

They part for me I walk right by them without shooting them another glance. I hear them whispering behind me, but I know it's nothing but a bunch of hogwash coming out of their mouths. Next time they see someone like me, they'll think twice before trying anything.

The further I get from them, the more my heart calms down. Finally. I can't believe it went that well. The back of my mind was preparing for a brawl, figuring out the best ways to take each of them down. Luckily, it didn't come to that.

Oh Lord, if only my mom could see me now: walking through Third Ward with a Glock strapped to my waist. She'd never believe it. I don't know if I fully believe it right now. But it's happening. And I've survived… at least so far.

***

Trails of sweat continue running down my arms and neck. I will never get used to this Texas heat. I make it to the area behind the townhouse without any more incidents. Thankfully, I don't cross paths with anything else: humans or animals. The only people I saw were a handful of women that were too far to be any trouble. That's the way I intend to keep it.

Even so, my heart rate is still beating rather quickly. It's not as bad as when I walked into that pack of gangbangers, but it's still far from normal. And my nerves are just as bad. The entire way here, I keep having the sensation that somebody is stalking me and that I'm being watched. But every time I look behind me, there's nothing there. The echo of my footsteps seems to be getting my nerves excited. Dear God, please let that be the case.

On the backside of the complex is an abandoned gas station. It's been out of commission for some time now. The grass is overgrown, and there are weeds everywhere. The windows are all reinforced with metal bars as can be expected, but many of them are cracked or smashed up. The walls are weathered along with the paint, which is only a shadow of its original self. The entire infrastructure seems to be falling apart. The store's sign is gone, but it's easy to see where it once stood. The inside of the store is nothing but empty shelves. It looks like even the light bulbs have been stolen, making it all mirror the scene from a post-apocalyptic movie.

There doesn't seem to be a reason for anybody to come near here. But it's just what I need. Turning toward the ancient tree that's casting its shadow on the forgotten store, I make my way there. The tree holds countless branches—many of them sturdy and thick—making it the perfect place to watch the townhome from.

I perform one final sweep to make sure that there's nobody nearby. It looks like I'm in the clear. With my messenger back still hanging off of my shoulder, I reach up and grab the lowest trunk of the tree. I easily pull myself up onto it. As I do, memories of my childhood flash through my mind. Angela and I climbed trees all the time. We would sit in the branches for hours while drawing, telling stories, and reading novels. The flood of nostalgia overruns my thoughts as I relive those golden days.

I never imagined it would be a skill I'd use to bring down criminals. I come onto the first branch before continuing higher. I scale with ease, having climbed trees hundreds of times before. With my foot firmly on the first branch, I grab the second and pull myself up onto it. I do the same with the third without missing a beat. Tree climbing is something that has never been tiring to me. If anything, it was one of the best ways to clear my mind. I step up onto the fourth branch as I reach up and grab the next one. It's thinner than the others but should hold my w—

It breaks.

Oh, God! It all happens in slow motion. Still holding the broken branch, I feel myself falling downwards. Instinctively, I grab the nearest one with my free hand. My entire body weight suddenly goes onto my hand, but I somehow hold on as my body violently lurches to a stop. I let go of the broken branch and watch as it falls onto the tall grass below. Hanging with one hand, I look away from the fallen branch and back up toward where I need to go. My palms sweat like crazy. I take a deep breath and let it out.

Calm down, Ana. It's just a hiccup. Keep moving.

Letting out a low groan, I reach up, and my second hand grabs ahold of the branch before I pull myself up onto it as if I'm doing a pull-up at the gym. Coming onto the branch, I stand on it while holding onto the tree trunk. I let out a few more breaths, calming myself down. Again looking down at the fallen branch, I know that could have easily been me. But it's not. My gaze returns to my destination. Almost there.

I scale one more branch higher, just to ensure I'm out of sight. The last thing I need is to be seen while I'm keeping tabs on the townhouse. I make it there with no more problems and take a seat on it, leaning my back against the trunk. It's more than sturdy enough to hold my weight and there are enough branches and leaves around me to keep me shrouded. My vantage point gives me a perfect view of the target. I should be safe here.

I do a quick scan of the tree to make sure there aren't any other occupants here. The main thing I'm worried about is snakes. Garden Snakes won't be a problem since their bite hurts less than sandpaper, but a Copperhead would be a very different story. However, the only thing here are a few flies buzzing around me, but I don't mind them. Better them than snakes. Or even worse, mosquitoes. I can't stand those bloodsuckers.

Taking a deep breath, I wipe the sweat off of my brow. After all this is over, I'm going to need a cold shower. A nice and *long* cold shower. But that will come later. Right now, all I need to do is sit and wait. The hardest part of all this is over. At least, I'm hoping.

The building is hard to see in detail from here, but my camera can zoom in and see the building clear as day. I quickly whip the device out of my bag and bring it to my face. I focus the lens onto the back of the building and do a quick scan of it. The rear appears just as bad as the front, weathered and unkempt. It seems like all the windows have their blinds closed—

My heart skips a beat.

One of the window's thick blinds is not fully closed, giving me a small peephole into the townhouse. It's only a crack, almost too small to give anything away. But with my camera, I can get a glimpse of the building's interior.

I focus the camera on the crack and zoom is as far as it'll go until my entire vision is solely on it. There's nothing there now, except for the room's wall. But I have all the time in the world. If there is something, I'll see it in no time... hopefully.

***

This is the longest hour of my life. I feel like a stalker sitting up here in a tree and watching the window through my camera. Outside of a few stray cats walking by and the flies buzzing around me, there's been nothing to report. Nothing has entered into view except for the bare wall I've been staring at for God knows how long.

My heart has calmed down since settling on this branch. Sitting up here and actually doing the reconnaissance work feels a bit surreal. It's like I'm in one of those spy movies, watching the enemy. I bet I could even teach James Bond a lesson or two about spying. But then again, I don't think he'd be caught dead in a down-ridden area like this.

As much as I try to keep focused on the townhouse, my mind continues to wander. The main thing I'm concerned about is what somebody would think if they saw me up here in this tree. Probably that I'm some ex-girlfriend stalking their former man. At least, that's what I hope they'd think. Otherwise, things could get rather complicated.

At first, I attempt to swat at the flies buzzing around me. But it doesn't take me long to give up on that. They don't bite. And I'd rather be dealing with them than anything that does bite. A nice long shower after all this will get rid of anything they leave on me. Oh God, a cold shower sounds *so* nice right about now.

It's scorching. And being in this tree seems to make it even hotter. The humidity is just icing on the already unbearable cake. Streams of sweat run down my face and body. I wipe myself down with the towel from my messenger bag a few times, but now it's drenched as well. And the thought that Bryan is probably sitting in the car with the A/C blasting while I'm up in this hellhole makes my blood start to boil. I picture him smiling to himself as he stares at the townhome through a pair of binoculars or something. He could've done this as easily as me. I'm sure he knew exactly what he was doing when he sent me out here. I swear, next time I see him, I'll—

What's that? Looking through my camera lens, I see a figure finally come into view through the window's small slit. *Please don't be daydreaming, Ana.* After a long moment, I'm sure I'm not seeing things. Somebody is really there.

His back is turned to me. The back of his head looks just like Moore's, but I can't be sure. I barely notice something on the right side of his neck. It's hard to tell, but from what I see, it can easily be the tattoo that Moore has.

My heart starts to quicken its pace. This time, it's not caused by fear. Instead, it's from excitement. As I push the camera harder against my face, my hand starts to tremble a bit, but I quickly regain control over it.

Turn around, Moore.

Is he talking to someone? Looks like it, but I can't see the other figure. My heart begins beating faster—and faster—and faster with anticipation. It feels like it'll burst out of my chest at any moment now. And as my heart rate spikes, my breaths instinctively start to quicken as well.

Come on, turn around already.

He's still talking. I press my face into the camera, as if looking harder at him will make him turn around. Yeah, that tattoo is definitely the one he had in the photo. It's got to be him.

Look my way, Moore. Just for a second.

He doesn't. He keeps the back of his head facing me and continues speaking to somebody. The longer it takes, the faster my heart races. I'm going to get a heart attack waiting for this punk to turn around. For the love of God, just look my way for one second. He stops talking. At least, it looks like he does.

Wait, is he doing it? This could be it.

Yes! He slowly turns his head so that I can see the right side of his face. I press down on my camera's trigger and it takes nearly ten photos in quick succession. He continues turning his head until he's nearly facing my way. I keep my finger pressed down on the button and my camera continues capturing countless images, one right after the other. And as it does, I find myself staring right at the face of Raheem Moore.

Bingo!

He looks just like his picture. The only difference now is his hairdo. I'm too far for him to be able to see me. But I've gotten more than enough looks at him. I quickly place my camera back into my bag as I whip out my radio. Pressing the button, I bring it close to my face. "You there?"

There's brief static. *"Shoot."*

"I got what we came for."

Bryan is silent for a long moment. *"Great job. Where are you?"*

"In a tree directly behind the compound."

"Go to the corner on your left. I'll pick you up there."

"Got it."

Putting the radio away, I sling my bag over my shoulder and begin to scale down. As difficult as climbing a tree is, it can sometimes be more difficult coming down. But today, I have no problems and don't miss a step as I head toward the ground. My excitement seems to make my instincts even sharper. Stepping onto the lowest branch, I do a small jump and perfectly land crouched down.

I rise to my feet and dust off some debris from my pants. I've made it. I survived the mission. I can't believe it—

"What were you doin' up in tha' tree?"

I freeze. For a long moment, I can't move and feel some color leave my face. *Please don't be happening. Not now when I'm so close to being in the clear.* I slowly turn around and arrive face-to-face with the source of the voice: a man. He's large and overweight, but his posture says that he can handle himself. His face is gruff, his hair long. His eyes display remnants of drugs. There's not even three feet between us. How the hell did I not see him?

I realize what's in his hands: a knife. Oh, crap.

"I saw you up there in tha' tree. I was waitin' for you to come down."

How the hell did I not see this idiot? You let your guard down, Ana. Think fast.

"How-a-bout you give me your bag?"

The bag has my camera. My gaze goes from his knife and back onto his face. *C'mon Ana, think.*

His eyes travel up and down my body. "Bag now missy… or I'll be taking more than that."

I slowly sling the bag off of my shoulder. His focus stays on it. I would give it to him without a fight under any other circumstances, if only to keep my cover. But I need the camera. He has his knife out, and its tip is pointed directly at my guts. He's too close for me to go for my gun without risking it. He's too big for me to take down in a fair fight, even without his knife. *Think, Ana. Where's my advantage?* The bag's strap is off my shoulder and in my hand now.

I got it.

Raising the bag up an inch, I break the silence. "This bag?"

"Yea." He reaches out for it. "Nice 'n slow now."

"Here ya go."

I don't think. I swing the bag like a mace and it slams right into his face. He stumbles backward, dropping the knife as he does. He's completely dazed and spits out some blood. I step up and cock my leg back before slamming it right into his stomach. He roughly falls backward and onto the overgrown grass, groaning as he does.

He's mine now. I give him a good, swift kick to the head with everything I've got. The thug's lights go out.

I take a deep breath as I turn around. Slinging the messenger bag back across my shoulder, I leave the unconscious mugger behind. I wish I could arrest him. But that would blow everything. At least he's learned his lesson. Just like those other punks, he'll think twice next time he's about to mess with somebody.

CHAPTER 8
THE BUST

"What have we got?"

As we drive back toward the highway, I rummage through my messenger bag. Being in this car, safe from the outside world, finally gives my heart and mind a rest. Pulling the camera out of my bag, I examine it. The lens is shattered while the focus rings and f-stops broke clean off, but the rest is still intact. "Moore was there. I got a pic to prove it—actually I got a lot of pics... but I may have busted the camera. Film is okay though."

Bryan raises his eyebrows. "...broke the camera?"

"It's a story."

"Is it worth telling?"

"Maybe some other time. Unless you want to hear about me using it to club some punk down. But I'm sure you had more exciting stuff happen to you while you were sitting in the car for an hour."

He slightly smiles. "Thank God we're not paying for the camera. They cost a fortune."

"I bet they do." I take a deep breath, feeling my heart finally settle back at its normal pace. I can see the highway from here. "So what's the plan?"

"Get back to HQ. I'll contact Judge Bradley about the warrant. Even without the photo, your word should be enough to get it. But the photos will definitely seal the deal. We'll have SWAT raid the place as soon as possible."

"Will we be there?"

"I'll be there overseeing it, but I want you to go home."

"Bryan—"

"You've had a rough day. I know it took a lot out of you. Take a breather and a cold shower. I got a glimpse of the personnel at the stash house. Raid should go down like clockwork."

I want to be there when it all goes down, but I don't have the energy to argue right now. I'm too exhausted to do that. "Whatever you say."

***

I get home a little past lunchtime. As Bryan suggested, I take a cold shower. The water rinses everything away: the dirt, stench, sweat, and even the nerves—at least for a little while. Not planning on going anywhere for the rest of the afternoon, I have the rest of the day to myself. I finally realize how famished I am with the mission now over and the adrenaline gone. The entire time I'm in the shower, my stomach continuously growls and clenches down on itself.

Dressed in some comfortable work-out clothes, I open up the fridge. Dang it, I haven't gone grocery shopping in far too long. The fridge is nearly bare, except for some milk, juice, and a few vegetables. I look down at a bag of carrots. Well, beggars can't be choosers.

Grabbing a handful of carrots, I make my way toward Angela's memorial across from my bedroom. I make a mental note to grab some groceries before the day is up. I crunch down on one of the carrots as I walk, quickly chewing and swallowing the mouthful. Can carrots go bad? Because these taste a bit off.

As always, the room is just as I left it. I stare at the wall covered in the web of facts and slowly make my way there. I stop a foot away from it and stare at Angela's face. She is as beautiful as ever in this picture. Her smile says everything about her. It shows her love, compassion, and genuine heart. She was everything I hoped to be.

But that was a long time ago.

90

They never could find out who her murderers worked for. Police knew the drive-by happened on the orders of a drug cartel, but the shooters refused to say which cartel they were a part of, even when the DA offered to cut off some jail time. But I bet the shooters knew that most of them would get off easy being minors. They must've had no problems keeping their mouths shut.

I take a step back. My vision slowly widens out from Angela's face and onto the entire web. Based on who the shooters were and their weapons, I know they belonged to one of the city's larger cartels. But there are quite a few of those, so knowing that doesn't help much. However, from researching where the shooters lived, I was able to narrow it down to three cartels: Free Streets, The Brotherhood, or *Los Famila.* Outside of that, I could never find anything else. At least, nothing strong enough to be taken as a fact.

Maybe that's why I took this job. Maybe I thought that somewhere along the line, I'll find something or someone who could help me piece everything together. The odds of that are almost one against infinity... but maybe the hope of one day finding the one responsible for Angela's death is what has kept me going all these years. Even if it is only a glimmer of hope, it is still hope. After all, without hope, what do we have?

Knock! Knock!

Thrown out of my trance, I instinctively whip my head around and in the direction of the front door. Who could that be? I never get any visitors. I leave Angela's memorial and quickly make my way toward my apartment's entrance.

Knock! Knock! "Ana, are you there?"

Ramon? Why the heck is my brother here?

I immediately grab my gun off of the kitchen counter and hide it away in a drawer. Arriving at the door, I swiftly unlock and open it. Sure enough, Ramon is standing on the other side. Dressed in a pair of blue jeans and a polo shirt, he smiles when he sees me. "Hey, sis."

"Hey, Ramon, what's up?"

"Laura and I were just passing by and were thinking about you."

"Laura? Where is she?"

"In the car." Ramon motions to his parked car in the lot behind him. "We were actually about to grab some lunch. Interested in joining us?"

Having lunch with somebody else is the last thing I want to do right now. I can't get my mind off of the bust about to happen and just want to get some rest. Maybe even some sleep if my mind will allow it. "Uhh... well, Ramon, I think I'll take a rain check today. I'm tired—"

"C'mon, Ana." He playfully nudges my shoulder like he would when we were kids. "Don't bail out on us. We only ever see each other at church these past few weeks."

"I'm really not feeling it, Ramon."

"I won't take 'no' for an answer. And I won't leave until you come with us."

Knowing him, he's telling the truth. He would literally stand at my door for hours unless I come with him. I let out a defeated sigh. "Alright. Let me get dressed."

***

Right now, Bryan is overseeing the raid on the stash house. I visualize it all in my mind's eye. Heavily armed SWAT teams break down the front and back door simultaneously, charging in with their weapons raised and ordering everyone inside to drop their weapons. Bryan is watching everything from afar or maybe even leading the charge himself, wearing a black ski mask over his face. The dealers are surrendering and dropping their weapons without a fight.

With the chaos over, Bryan walks up to the defenseless Moore and puts the handcuffs on the murderer himself. I hear Bryan reading Moore his rights. Maybe he even adds in a line about the people Moore murdered in cold-blood.

It's as if I'm there myself.

"…Ana?"

Snapping out of my spell, I look up at Laura. Reality sinks back in. In a diner, I'm sitting across the table from Ramon and his wife. We're in the corner booth, away from prying eyes. I notice the worry in their gazes. Oh, God, how long was I daydreaming for?

"Are you okay?"

"Yeah. Yeah, sorry." I've got to get ahold of myself. "Just had some things on my mind."

"Is anything bothering you?" Ramon asks.

"Nothing to be worried about. I was just thinking about a friend."

"You're so distant nowadays. Seriously, if there's anything bothering you—"

"I'm fine, Ramon. Really."

After a long moment, Ramon nods.

The waitress brings out our beverages and sets them in front of us before leaving without a word. Looking down at my Sprite, I take a quick sip of it as Laura breaks the uneasy silence. "How's the new job?"

I clear my throat. "Doesn't feel too new anymore."

My brother slightly smiles. "Is the life of a receptionist already getting boring?"

"It has its high moments. You'd be surprised."

Ramon takes a long sip of his iced tea. "Filing papers and answering calls? That must be absolutely exuberating."

If only he knew. If only anyone knew. But they can't. Right now, Ramon is thinking that I spent my day in an office, filing papers and answering phone calls. He doesn't know where I've been or what I've seen. Nobody knows that it wasn't too long ago that Miller tried to gut me for a quick buck. Nobody knows that even today I faced plenty of scenarios that could have easily gone the wrong way. And nobody in hell knows that after all these years I'm still trapped in the past, unable to accept Angela's death.

But that's the way it'll stay. Because this is my burden. And there are some burdens that you just have to face… alone.

"So, Ana when—"

Beep!

Everyone's eyes go onto the pager hanging from my waist. I quickly rise to my feet without hesitating.

"Are you leaving?" Ramon asks, eyebrows raised.

"That's my… uh, boss. He's the only one who has that number. I need to make a call."

"I thought you were off work."

"Must be an emergency."

"Can't it wait until after?"

"Sorry, I'll be back in a jiffy."

"R—Really?"

"Yeah. Just give me a minute."

***

The diner's phone is preoccupied, so I quickly find a payphone on the street corner. Inserting my quarter, I punch in the number for Bryan's office. I impatiently tap my foot against the ground as I wait for the ringing to begin. It rings once. Then twice. Then—

"Bryan Fulton."

"It's me. How did it all go down?"

"Perfectly."

Hearing that simple word, I feel a weight roll off of my chest. I barely stop myself from doing a fist pump in the air.

"It all went down like clockwork. Two teams of SWAT went in. One from the front and one from the back. We went in heavy. I went in with the front team. When we went in, the dealers were in total shock. They couldn't even get off a single shot. It didn't even take three minutes to get them all in handcuffs."

"How many were there?"

"Three, not including Moore. And there were ten kilos of goods in the stash house, all the way from crack to cocaine."

"Ten kilos?"

"I didn't believe it until I saw it."

"That's amazing." I take a moment to soak in what Bryan is telling me. The entire operation went down perfectly. Unbelievable. "What about Moore?"

"We nailed him. He surrendered without a fight. I got to put the cuffs on him myself. There's no way he'll be getting out of this, not after all the people he's hurt. They're interrogating him now. Do you want to listen in?"

I pause for a long second. I most certainly do want to be there, but there's the little problem of my brother and sister-in-law waiting for me in the diner. I shouldn't. It'll only arouse suspicion. I know that. But… maybe I can get them to understand. "Yeah, I'll be heading over in a minute."

***

Ramon and Laura aren't too excited to hear that I've been called in for work. Who can blame them? But they buy the lie. Neither tries to argue with me and they let me go without a fight.

Moore is grilled about his cartel. He doesn't say anything about it that officers didn't already suspect, including the fact that he's a part of *Los Familia*. The interrogator is a good one and he pulls all the tricks of the trade, but Moore doesn't budge. Whomever Moore is working for has him scared. From the look in Moore's eyes, that's no easy task.

The figure at the head of *Los Familia* is somebody with a lot of power. And a part of me thinks that it is somebody who will cause us a lot of problems.

With Moore locked up, I sense a feeling of closure in Bryan, at least for this chapter in his life. Zhen Hue's killer, along with the murderer of several citizens, will finally face justice. If nothing else, at least the family of the dead will have some kind of solace.

***

Some days, Bryan and I work the streets together. But other times, we both operate as lone wolves. It's been almost a month—or maybe it's been over a month—since I went from jailor to officer. I'm sad to say that I've forgotten the exact date I received the badge.

I haven't had any informants call in over the past few days, leaving me to simply drive around to all the hotspots in my area to see if any dealers approach me. Bryan was tipped this morning about a possible dealer who we'd been on the lookout for. I offered to go with him, but he said the informant was typically unreliable so he'd check it out on his own.

Taking the exit off of Beltway 8, I spot a run-down gas station just off the road. And parked at one of the pumps is a dirty, beat-up Toyota Corolla with shining rims. I take a deep breath upon seeing it.

Well, it's worth a shot.

I switch on my indicator to pull into the gas station. My car comes to a halt at the pump opposite to the beat-up car's. The fair-skinned man has his back turned to me. Wearing a pair of baggy shorts and a shirt that's two sizes too big, he watches the meter go up as he fills his car.

With my Glock concealed in my back pocket, I switch my vehicle off and step out of it. The one thing that always worries me about my gun is that it doesn't have a safety. Of all the ways to die on this job, accidentally shooting yourself is not the most heroic way to go.

Feeling a presence behind him, the man turns his head and sees me standing on the other side of our parallel cars. He catches my slight smile, and after a long moment, he returns the gesture. But as I finally see his face, I can't help but feel that there's something strikingly familiar about him.

"What's up, girl?" he says as he fully turns around to look at me.

"What's up wit' you, handsome?"

96

"Tryin' to make money."

"You work somewhere close?"

"I do, but I ain't got a job."

"What you do?"

"I got a buzi-nez."

Jackpot! When my mom told me that you attract certain people by the way you dress, she definitely wasn't lying. He wouldn't have said that if I was dressed and talking the way I normally do. And the state of my dirty undercover vehicle is only icing on the cake for why he's so candid. "My neighbor got a buzi-nez too," I reply. "Maybe you got the same kind."

"What kind he got?"

"He sells stones. But he a rip-off."

He pauses as if he's taken aback by my forwardness. "Your neighbor?"

I nod.

"What's his name?"

I say the name with all the conviction in the world. "O. W."

He immediately buys it. "Well, if you lookin' for a better deal, I got it."

"I'm lookin' if you're offerin'." *So far so good.*

The man doesn't reply. Not right away, at least. It's a long enough silence to make the situation awkward. And the stillness makes me start to feel uneasy. Weird. His eyes slowly change for the worse as his smile disappears. They tell me this situation just took a nosedive. There is suddenly a strong presence of suspicion, and ill-intentions manifest behind it. His voice changes with his expression. "Ya know, you look like someone I seen before."

If this is his way of hitting on me, then it's a really weird way of doing it, but I play along by letting out a girlish laugh. "I get that a lot."

He doesn't share my amusement. "Seriously, there was this girl I met—a jailor."

Oh, s—

"I 'waz locked up in county and she was there." He takes one small step closer. "You look jus' like her."

The memories suddenly flood in. Holy crap, he's right. This man—Nate Hopkins—was arrested for a DUI and locked up in county for a few days before he paid his bail. *Keep your composure, Ana.* "I don't know no jailors."

He squints his eyes as if that'll make him remember my face better. "You look just like her."

"When were you in county?"

"Two years ago."

"Two years is a long time."

"Yea', but I don't forget faces. Especially one as pretty as hers... and yours."

I see one of his hands reach toward his side. He's got a gun. Crap.

"She was a real hard-ass," he continues. "I swore that if I ever saw her again—"

Think fast, Ana. "You think I'm her?"

Nate's hand creeps closer to his concealed gun.

My eyes are in sync with my character and suddenly fill with disgust. I spit out my next words. "My brother and my sister are both locked up for life and you call'n me a cop! You better take that back before I break your damn legs."

He hesitates for a moment. *C'mon, back off.* If he touches his gun, it'll be a race to draw first. He doesn't know I'm packing. By the time he does, I'll make sure it's too late for him to do anything. But drawing my gun will blow my cover. And the last thing I need is a corpse instead of a bust.

Nate's hesitation doesn't last and he touches his gun through his shirt.

I need to get him to back off. Quickly. *Think, Ana. Think.* He hasn't pulled his gun out so he's not fully sure of himself. There's still a chance. If you believe what you're saying, he'll believe it too.

98

"Keep touching tha' gun and you'll be on the ground pumped full of lead."

The warning doesn't cause him to waver. "That a threat?"

"A promise. I roll with Ant."

"…who?"

I make the name up on the spot. But I speak with enough conviction that even a lie detector would believe me. "Antonio Juarez. Arms dealer in Cypress. You mess with me, then you mess with his family and him. And there ain't nothing more importan' to him than family."

There is a long moment of silence as Nate blankly stares at me. I see his fingers slightly back off of his gun. I've got him. All I need to do is hammer the nails into the coffin and I'll have his trust.

"You remember that jailor's name?"

"…last name was Rocha."

"Rocha? Hell of a strange name." Quickly figuring out my next few moves, I reach into my back pocket and whip out my driver's license—the fake one. I feel his gaze burning on my face as I toss it toward him.

Nate easily catches it with one hand. After a long moment of staring at me, his gaze shifts down onto the card. He silently and subtly mouths the name on there: Isabel Garcia. His eyes go back and forth between the name and picture on the license before he finally looks up at me.

"I could've sworn…"

I stay silent.

He holds the license up to the sunlight, acting as if that'll help him determine if it's real or not. But after a few seconds, his focus returns to me and he tosses the license my way. I catch it without breaking my gaze with him and slide it back into my pocket. End this already. "You happy? Or you gonna keep wastin' more of my time? There are plenty of homies out there who'd be happy to work with me."

"Sorry… just had to be sure. Been to prison once. I ain't takin' no mo' chances. Queen Bee was pretty ticked when I did go and she let me know it when I got out."

Thank God. "It's coo'. I ain't got nothin' to hide."

I can end this now. Just hop in my car and drive off. It's already a tricky situation and one false move is all it'll take for him to realize that I am the jailor he thought I was. The sensible part of me wants to get out of here. But the other part wants me to keep pushing. And sadly, this job has taught me to listen to this part of my brain.

"So, how much for a bill?"

***

"You're serious?" Sitting across his office desk, Bryan's eyes are wide with awe. "He recognized you as the jailor—was actually about to pull his gun out—and you not only got him to back down but *still* got him to set up an exchange with you for tomorrow?"

I simply nod with a grin spread across my face.

He slams his hand onto his desk with excitement. "Wait until Mark hears this!"

I can't help but laugh at Bryan's amusement.

My partner leans back in his chair, shaking his head in disbelief. "You're too good, Ana."

"I'm glad to see you're so happy about me almost getting shot."

"Being 'almost shot' is part of the job. I'll cry you a river when you actually do get shot."

"That's very reassuring. By the way, I heard a name I didn't recognize."

"Shoot."

"Queen Bee."

"Queen Bee? That's the street name of the lady who runs most of the drug volume in South Houston. *Los Familia* is the name of her cartel."

"I've heard the name of that gang."

"Queen Bee owns a lot of local businesses, but it's all a front for her cartel. Moore was a member of her organization. So was Miller. The dealer you met works for her?"

I nod. "What's her real name?"

"Ebony Thorne."

"Why isn't she locked up?"

"The FBI has been after her for a while. They know where she lives—everyone knows where she lives. It's half an hour west of Houston. I could even take you there if you like. But they can't get anybody to confess against her and we have nothing to arrest her on. They've tried everything and so has HPD, but nobody can ever get any hard proof that she's the head of *Los Familia*."

"Maybe we can get the dealer I tagged today to confess?"

"I doubt it. She keeps her dealers and suppliers scared. And most of the people you'll come across who work for her don't know anything that could be of real use." After a quick silence, Bryan changes the topic. "So, tonight."

"What about tonight?"

"You have any plans?"

"I don't have a life, Bryan. You know that."

"Which is why I took the liberty of making a reservation over at Brenner's Steakhouse for 7:30pm."

"...what's the occasion?"

"It's your one-month anniversary today. Or have you forgotten?"

I'm slow to respond. "I guess I have... is this something worth celebrating with steaks?"

"Well, you haven't died or quit yet. So yeah, I think it is."

CHAPTER 9
THE LINE

It's a pretty nice joint. Not a five-star place and not somewhere you'd catch James Bond eating, but not a cheap dump either. The waiter seems to know Bryan well. At least well enough that he gives us a free appetizer. You can't go wrong with lobster shrimp.

Bryan is wearing a pair of black slacks and a dark grey blazer over his white dress shirt. I never imagined he would clean up so nicely. But I don't look too shabby myself in my knee-length and short-sleeved, emerald green dress. My partner gets a twelve-ounce sirloin and insists that I buy nothing less than a filet. It doesn't take much persuasion for me to comply.

The restaurant is mostly empty as it nears closing time. I'm not a drinker, but I can't say the same for Bryan. He puts it down quickly and has had a bit much in the way of drinks as our meal closes. Some people tend to start slurring their words when they get intoxicated, while others become bipolar. But it seems the more he drinks, the only thing that happens to Bryan is that he grows more open.

Setting his nearly empty glass of wine back on the table, he looks at me. "So how does your one-month-anniversary feel?"

I think about it for a moment. "Same as my first day. Only scarier."

"Being scared is good. It keeps you alive." Bryan glances down at his bottle. "And in our line of work, not everybody makes it out alive. Sometimes it's your best friends who die." His gaze returns to me. "I'm sure you've figured out what happened to my last partner."

I almost don't know if it's appropriate for me to answer that question. I'm not sure if he even wants a response. But my reply rolls right off my tongue. "...what was his name?"

"Jack... Jack Wise." A slight smile forms on Bryan's face as countless memories flash in his eyes. "He was a total pain in the ass when we first met. He'd only been in the force for two years when I joined up as a young hotshot. Saying that we didn't get along at first is putting it lightly. I almost asked for a new partner after our second week together. Sound familiar?"

I smirk without replying.

"But our work made us soldiers-in-arms. And we soon became brothers. He was the best man at my wedding and was there for the birth of my child. He was the second person to hold my son after me. We were best friends. Our weeks would go by together at work, and our weekends would comprise of fishing and camping." He takes a deep breath. "Those were the days... the best days..."

There is a pause.

"But one day, he went out to meet an informant—a trusted one. It was routine. I asked him if he wanted back-up. Something made me insist. Something inside told me not to let him go alone. He declined and I let him go without a fight... but he never came back. His body was found two days later. He'd been stabbed seven times and left to bleed out in some gutter."

Bryan utters those words with complete disgust before looking down.

"They never caught the killer. Nobody except officers attended the funeral. Outside of my wife, everyone there was from the force. His parents were dead. He didn't have any friends." He takes another deep breath. "But that's what this job does to you, Ana. It sucks the life out of you and then leaves you for dead. It makes you live two lives and you have to fight *every second* of *every day* for them not to cross into one another. But one day, you'll find yourself letting go of your civilian life—

letting go of everyone and everything you hold dear and fully embracing this… this darkness."

I don't know if I should ask the next question, but I can't stop myself. "Is that what happened to you?"

Bryan solemnly nods. "Before this job, I didn't do… this." He holds up his glass. "I had a bright personality… just like you. I was a completely different man. I was the man that my wife fell in love with."

"Does she know?"

"Mary knows what I do for a living. But even still, our relationship went downhill right after marriage because of this job. Our son is the only reason we didn't get a divorce. But one day, she told me that she needed time away. Worst part is that she took our son." He shuts his eyes for a moment. "That was four months ago… six months after Jack's death. It's what this line of work does. It kills you or it leaves you dead inside. And when your death does come, you die alone. There's nobody to mourn you except for the comrades you leave behind."

I remain silent.

"And no matter what we do, no matter how hard we fight, we can *never* win. For every criminal we lock up, another pops up to take their place. No matter how many screws we take out, we can't stop the machine. Nobody cares about the sacrifice we make. The public seems to despise our uniform no matter what. It's like we're not even human to them. We can never be good enough. Bad cops make the headlines while good cops are cast aside without a second thought."

There is an uneasy stillness before he continues.

"You want some real advice, Ana? Get out. Get out of this while you still can."

***

Nate Hopkins does get locked up. However, like Bryan predicted, he doesn't say a word against Ebony Thorne. Turns out, most of the dealers I've been busting work for the same cartel—*Los Familia*—but none of them ever confess. Bryan wasn't exaggerating when he said Ebony keeps her people trapped in a clench of fear.

Days turn into weeks. Bryan and I continue our one-two-punch combo. The more we work together, the more he starts to open up. He tells me about his childhood, his son, and, occasionally, his wife. His son just started playing Little League and turned six a few days ago, but Bryan did not attend the birthday party.

And in return, I tell him about myself. The more we learn about each other, the better we become in our work. Bryan and I seem to possess the same kind of relationship I have with my own brother. We're from two different worlds, but our duty links us together.

We average three or four deals a week, which is double the average for the normal narcotics officer. Cap loves it. Mark Davidson hates it. He tries to push my buttons every once in a while, making excuses as to why I'm experiencing success. He says it's because I'm a woman or because I'm Hispanic. But the truth is simpler than that.

Bryan and I are simply better at our jobs.

The more time that passes, the more I hear about Queen Bee from the dealers I come into contact with. But even though they're in her organization, none of them possess any real dirt on her. All the dealers we make exchanges with are busted within two to four weeks after the exchanges. They plead guilty almost every time. However, none of them are willing to work with us to help bring *Los Familia* down, even after the promise of no jail time.

During these weeks and months, I start to compile my own list of suspected dealers that operate on our turf. I have our informants keep an eye out for them. And when they do spot them, I make contact and do what I can to bring them down. As time goes by, 'Ana's Most Wanted List' slowly shrinks in size. But every once in a while, I add another name to the list.

On the anniversary of my third month, I receive a letter from Texas' Attorney General congratulating me on my work. Apparently,

Captain Scott was bragging to his superior. My first instinct is to show it to my mother. I even pick up the phone to call her.

But then I remember. The life of Officer Rocha is separate from the life of Ana Rocha. Officer Rocha's life is full of guns, crime, and drugs. Ana's is full of smiles, warmth, and sunshine. The thing I fear more than anything is the day the line between them breaks and they mix. And with that fear in mind, I don't make the call.

***

Bryan's advice from my one-month anniversary hits home soon after I receive the congratulatory letter.

I jolt up from another nightmare. It's almost a nightly habit now. I'm drenched in my own sweat and my heart rate is out of control. The nightmare was just like the one that has been haunting my dreams for a while. There was chaos in the streets. Destruction surrounded me. And so did corpses.

Calming myself down after several moments, I finally get myself off of my bed. The morning routine goes like any other: brush my teeth, eat breakfast, and freshen up. But then I open my bedroom's closet.

And what I see makes my partner's words all the more clearer. As I stare at the numerous outfits hanging there, I notice something. Something that I've failed to notice before. It's been slowly happening over the past months, but I never realized it until now.

The clothes of Officer Rocha outnumber those of Ana.

CHAPTER 10
BRYAN

Bryan and I don't have any meets today, and none of our informants call either. That leaves us with only two options: paperwork or meeting 'new friends' at local hotspots. And for me and Bryan, there's only one right answer here. After some of the recent excitement, I don't mind the slower day. It's long overdue. A part of me hopes that we don't run into any potential dealers and end up just driving around town all day. Sometimes those are the best kinds of days.

As always, Bryan drives. He's the typical man who won't let anyone else drive his car no matter what. He could be in a full-body cast and coma, but still wouldn't let me even think about touching the wheel. This car is his kingdom. But what else can you expect from a good 'ole country boy like him?

I resign to simply staring out the window as we move along the famous 610 Loop. Everything inside is Houston, and everything outside the loop is a wanna-be-Houston. I look out at the towering skyscrapers of downtown and the Medical Center that nearly touch the clouds. Whenever it gets really cloudy, you can't even see the tops of these lofty buildings. Driving quietly with Bryan is always one of the best relaxers; in some ways, it's almost as effective as visiting Angela's tomb. Bryan usually lets me get lost in my thoughts and entertains himself with a sports channel or country music. Today is no different.

However, after a few minutes of a peaceful drive, he breaks the silence. "What did you think about the letter?"

Bryan's words bring me back into reality, causing me to look his way. "The Attorney General's?"

"You receive any other congratulatory letters lately?"

I slightly smile. "It was… unexpected. I didn't think he'd notice us little people."

"He normally doesn't. Actually, almost nobody does." He shoots me a glance. "But I think I would have appreciated a raise more than a letter. Or at least a bonus."

"I wouldn't get my hopes up too much for that."

"Yeah… a letter is probably as good as it'll get."

Bryan turns the car onto the exit for 59 South, which will lead us to Sugarland. With the suburb's building ordinances, you can hardly tell any of the red-bricked strip malls or buildings apart. Even with all the wealth in the city, it's not hard to find drug dealers in the suburb. But maybe the area's wealth is what attracts the dealers. Who knows?

The sports radio is lowly playing throughout the beat-down car. The last three days have been country music. It's made me sick to my stomach, so I'm grateful for the change-up today. Two men are going on about the Astros. Apparently, this 1999 season will be their last season in the Astrodome. Next year, they'll be playing in Enron Stadium. It sounds so weird for a stadium's name. Hopefully it doesn't stick too long.

As the regular season starts its final stretch over the next couple of months, it looks like the Astros have a good chance to edge out the Reds for the NL Central Division Title. But with the Astros, you can never count our marbles until it's all over. However, with people like Biggio playing the way they are, the Astros have a good chance to make a playoff run. I've never been much of a baseball person myself, but after listening to so many talk shows with Bryan, I know enough to debate an expert. I could probably hold my own against these two whack-jobs on the show right now.

The Houston skyscrapers are far behind us as we continue south toward Sugarland. The highway is mostly empty this time of day. During rush hour, this trek would take us nearly three times as long. Driving past a few empty baseball fields, I see Bryan cast them a long look.

"Missing your baseball days?" I ask.

"Oh, no." He focuses back on the road. "I only played because of my father. I was always more of a football man myself. Sadly, I could never really get Kevin into chasing pigskin. Believe me, I've been trying to turn him into a star quarterback ever since he could walk. He has a heck of an arm. But he loves baseball. Always has. All he ever talks about is Little League and the Astros. And he's good too."

Bryan hardly ever mentions his son, Kevin. Maybe it's because he's barely seen him these past few months, being that his son stays with Bryan's estranged wife.

"Kevin can pitch, field, and bat. That's a rare combination nowadays," Bryan continues. "Nobody on his team can even come close to him on anything."

"I'm sure he appreciates that."

"Appreciates what?" With a quick movement, he switches off the radio.

"You getting into baseball just for him. I take it that's why you listen to this talk show with those two goobers."

"It gives us something to talk about when I'm with him. At least for the few times I get to see him now." When he talks about his son or even mentions him, a joyful light flashes in Bryan's eyes.

I'm always hesitant to ask about his son, not wanting to stir anything up. But with him mentioning his son first, the moment feels right. "What's his team's name?"

"The Katy Sharks."

"How's his season going?"

"It's good... it's going good." Bryan doesn't look my way. "Kevin's team isn't much of a... well, team. Not too much support talent there. But he's the best player in the group. Definitely the most talented. Hardest working boy too."

"Have you been to any of his games?"

"I've watched them... but not from the stands." Bryan is quiet for a long moment. "I don't think my... uh, wife would appreciate me being there. And I want the games to be about him... not me."

"Does Kevin see you when you're there?"

Bryan nods as he slightly smiles. I can see memories of his son flashing through his eyes. "He loves it when he sees me. He puts that extra effort in when he notices me standing on the other side of the fence watching him. He dives for balls he otherwise wouldn't and runs faster than I've ever seen any kid run. He's carried them to some wins, but there's only so much one player can do."

"Just like how I carry *our* team."

Bryan's memories fade back into his mind as he grins at me. "Whatever helps you sleep at night, Ana."

"Trust me, I need all the sleep I can get these days."

His smile slowly disappears. "Trouble sleeping?"

"You could say that."

"Is it your sister?"

After Bryan's son, Angela is the second thing that's off-limits in our conversations. I've only ever mentioned her a few times before and each time was more of a vague reference than a statement. He's never really pushed about her. He's even gone as far as to not read the file on her, even though he has every right to as my partner. But I guess since I brought up Kevin, Bryan has the go-ahead to bring up my sister. "…sometimes it's her. Those are usually the worst nights."

"How often do you visit her grave?"

"Honestly, probably as often as you visit Jack's."

Hearing the name of his old partner, Bryan lets out a sigh. "That makes it too often."

I pause before replying, "Is that a thing? To visit a loved one's grave too much?"

"It can become an addiction. One that is almost impossible to break without losing your sanity."

"If that's the case, then I'm already addicted."

"That makes two of us, Ana." He lets out a soft sigh. "Two crazy people who can't stop flirting with death."

110

Those words are followed by a long silence. I don't think he meant to say those words; he just meant to think them. But the statement just rolled off of his heart before he could think twice. We keep to ourselves, not knowing what to say and reflecting on just how true Bryan's words are. It really would take an insane person to do what we do day in and day out.

After what feels like a long time, Bryan again breaks the peace. "Did she pass away when you were young?"

"She did."

"How old were you?"

"Old enough to remember every detail of the night."

"That's why you do this, isn't it?"

I simply nod.

"How did she die?"

"Wrong place, wrong time. She was gunned down in a drive-by shooting not meant for her. It was at a soup-kitchen she volunteered at every week." I don't know why I'm so open, but it all just feels right. Maybe now I've finally found someone I trust, or maybe I realize how much Bryan and I have in common when it comes to loss. "These punks came looking for a dealer who did their boss wrong and shot up the place. The man they came for didn't get a scratch. A few others get hurt." I pause for a long moment, reliving the night when the officer came to our home and I listened from the top of the steps. Every word I utter is filled with hate and disgust. "But Angela is shot close to her heart. She lies there, wounded for God knows how long... and chokes on her own blood."

Bryan remains silent.

"The same heart that she gave to so many people—the same heart that made her be at the soup kitchen in the first place—is the heart that killed her... ironic, isn't it?" I take a deep breath. "What's more ironic is knowing that her killers are not locked up in prison or sitting on death row like they should be. Instead, they get off easy while I'm left to pick up the pieces of the mess they made."

"...I'm sorry."

I act as if I don't hear his words. "They were... *juveniles*. So they were treated as such. But I don't doubt that their boss played a part in them getting free. The murderous scum lost a few days of their lives in prison while I lost my best friend."

There is no reply.

"I've spent every day since that night looking for an answer and looking for any sliver of solace. I've looked everywhere: family, church, and anywhere else I could outside of drugs and alcohol." With every word, more memories from that dreadful night flood my mind. I see the officer standing there, unable to offer any comfort to the pain his news brought down on my parents. I feel my heart bursting into tears again... and again... and again. For the first time, I learn what loneliness really is. And I feel helpless all over again. "But it seemed that even as everyone else moved on with their lives, I couldn't... and I still can't. Doing this—doing what we do—is the one way I can fill any of the holes in my heart."

There's a long minute of peace between Bryan and me. All that can be heard is the car's wheels as they beat against the cemented road. This is not how I thought this morning would go.

Finally, my words again break the stillness. "I can't move on, Bryan. I can't forget her. How could I? I want to break out of this prison... but I can't. All I can do is relive that night every day for the rest of my life."

Bryan's gaze leaves the road and falls upon me. He speaks so softly that I barely hear his words. "We can't bring back the dead, Ana. Not Jack or Angela. No matter how hard we pray or cry, the dead are just memories. And one day, those memories will fade. We won't remember how their voice sounded, and we won't remember what their companionship felt like. But what we can do is honor them. We can move forward and make their sacrifice worth something."

"I do honor her, Bryan. And you honor Jack too. We do it through our duty." I look straight ahead. "And I will keep doing it for as long as it takes."

***

This evening, like most evenings, I'm alone in my apartment, my thoughts acting as my only companion. There is a warm TV dinner in front of me, and my eyes are glued to a re-run of *X-Files*. But I'm not really paying it any heed. The things that the show claims to be 'strange' pale in comparison to some of the things I've seen. Or, more accurately, the people I've seen.

The whole day, I can't stop thinking about Bryan. The poor man is so hurt. He's dying a little bit every day. He loves his son, but can never see him. The closest he's come in these past few months is in photos and memories. Is that what I'm destined for as well? Maybe it is a part of this path and something that I will face sooner or later.

Is it too late for Bryan? I don't know if he is still holding onto any hope, but is the door to his family still even open to him? Could anything be done to undo the damage?

I wonder if…

Without thinking, I abruptly reach over for my phone and phonebook, nearly knocking over my cup of water as I do. I hold the phone in one hand while hastily searching through the directory. I quickly find the contact I'm looking for and swiftly punch in the number. I don't let my second thoughts get a chance to surface.

Putting the phone to my ear, I hear it ring a couple of times. I anxiously tap my fingers against the table. When the third ring sounds off, I start to think that maybe nobody's going to answer the—

"Katy City Hall."

"Yes, hi." I quickly gain my composure. "I was wondering if you could tell me where the Katy Sharks will be playing their next game."

***

I don't know what brings me here. Maybe the realization of my closet helped me comprehend exactly what Bryan was talking about. Or maybe it was hearing the sadness in my partner's voice when he talked about his son. But whatever the reason, it's brought me here on a bright and scorching Saturday morning. Instead of sleeping in like normal, I find myself pulling into a parking lot right outside a Little League baseball game.

Half of the crowd cheers as a kid races across home plate. The announcer's voice echoes through the stadium and parking lot. "A great run by Number 34, Kevin Fulton!"

Hearing those words tells me that I'm at the right place. Stepping out of my car, I head through the rusty gate and toward the stands. It's hot. Really hot. Even dressed in a pair of decent shorts, a short-sleeved shirt, and a baseball cap, I'm sweltering as if I'm entering Hell itself. But when you live in Texas, you just accept the heat as a fact of life. The game is in full swing now. Right after the last score, the next batter strikes out, putting the game in the bottom of the third inning. I see Bryan's son—Kevin—now in the outfield. Even from this distance, I notice the resemblance.

Both teams' parents share the same set of stands, which likely made watching this game much more entertaining. But I'm not here to enjoy baseball. Looking into the crowd, I see the person I've come to meet. She is sitting in the middle of the stands and is surrounded by other moms and dads. Even with her sunglasses and baseball cap on, I recognize the blonde-haired woman as Bryan's wife: Mary.

I casually make my way through the stands without being a distraction and take a seat next to her. But as I do, my heart starts to beat faster and faster. My palms begin sweating, and it's not from just the heat. I take a deep breath. This is my last chance to turn around and leave without making this whole thing awkward. But that option disappears when Mary looks at me and shoots a polite smile. I return the gesture before we both look out at the game. She watches it for enjoyment, but I do it because I can't think of a way to break the silence. I've gotten so good at breaking the ice and starting conversations with drug dealers that I've forgotten how to talk to normal people.

But she saves me the trouble when she speaks a couple of minutes later. "...so which one is your kid?"

Here's my chance. Let's do this, Ana. "I'm actually watching a friend's son."

"How nice. Who's their son?"

I look back in the outfield and point to Kevin. "Over there. Number 34."

I don't look back at her, but sense her smile disappear as she realizes who I am. It's apparent in her voice. "...oh."

Should have used a different approach, Ana. But her reaction is not nearly as bad as I thought it would be. Maybe it's just the calm before the storm. The entire inning passes in silence. Very awkward silence at that. I had rehearsed myself up to this point in the conversation, but never really thought I'd make it this far. Now, I'm not sure what to say.

The team's switch, and Kevin now sits in the dugout, waiting for his turn at bat. I start thinking that it was a mistake to have come here. The longer the silence runs, the worse I feel about all this. Maybe I didn't think this whole thing through. The last thing I want to do is ruin this mother's moment in seeing her son play baseball.

But then she again speaks. Mary's voice is harsher than it was before, which only makes the knot in my stomach tighten. "...did Bryan send you here?"

"No. But he's my friend and he talks about you all the time. He—" I pause for a second, knowing that I need to make my point quickly. "I don't think you know what's happening to Bryan right—"

"Bryan and I understand each other perfectly. He knows why I left. And he knows it's all for the best. It's better to get this all over with now rather than later." Her gaze leaves me and aims straight ahead. There is another awkward silence, but it quickly ends. And when she speaks, she keeps her focus on the field. "Are you happily married yourself?"

I don't reply.

"Then you can't understand the situation and you have no authority to make it your business." Mary pauses. "Please leave."

I blankly stare at her for a little while longer, but I know the truth. There's nothing I can do here. This was a mistake. She won't even hear a thing I say no matter how loud I shout it. And so without another word, I respect her wishes.

***

Sunday morning, I wake up from a nightmare. My sweat leaves the sheets a little damp. However, after all these nightmares, I hardly notice it anymore. I don't even take a moment to try and calm down my bewildered state. It's an hour before dawn, but I get out of bed. I know there's no sleeping now.

I go into the empty room—the one I've dedicated to Angela. Like I've done nearly every day, I sit against the wall that faces the web of facts. I keep my gaze on the grid, as if trying to find my solace in it. I know nothing good can come out of this staring, and I know that staring at it and reliving my sister's death over and over again only torments my soul.

But I can't stop myself.

I'm sitting there when the sun breaks the night's darkness. I'm still there when the phone starts ringing. Its echo reverberates through my apartment. But I don't flinch. And I don't make a move to answer it. I already know who it is.

For the past month and a half, I had been showing up to church late. Late enough that the only seats available were in the back row. Then, two Sundays ago, I left the church service early with an 'upset stomach'. And last Sunday, it was a 'serious headache' that forced me to leave prematurely. But both times, I just went and stayed in a bathroom stall until I heard the footsteps of the congregation out in the hallways.

It's already made my family suspicious, and I'm running out of excuses. But I can't stand the service. Every time the pastor speaks, it feels as if he's looking right at me. Especially when he is warning about the sins of lying. And for some reason, the topic seems to come up in every sermon. It's as if the Bible and my soul are telling me two different things. This duty is feeding my soul—it's filling the hole that Angela left. But my religion tells me that I am living in a lie. Maybe it is God. Maybe He is angry at me and is trying to pull me away from all of this. Or maybe it's just my own guilt.

So today, I did something that I haven't done in over a decade— something I never dreamed of doing as a child: I skipped church. And no doubt, on the other end of that line is a concerned mother. But she'll have to wait. As much as it pains me, I can't pick up the phone. I've ignored God and my mother in one day.

Both firsts for me.

***

Three days later, I'm sitting in my undercover car outside of a project. I would have fried to a crisp while waiting for this dealer to show up if it wasn't for my A/C. In Texas, we appreciate just how God-sent air conditioning really is.

It's already 20 minutes past the meeting time and this punk hasn't shown up. But that's not really a surprise. A week ago, two Indian looking medical students with funny sounding names—I think they were Mirza and Avinash—visiting Houston for the summer spotted a known dealer, Marco Flores, working the streets. After they called and told us where they'd spotted him, it was not hard for me to 'run into' him and set up a deal.

This morning, I again woke up with another nightmare. I don't know what's going on. For the past months since I became a cop, almost half my nights end with me waking up drenched in a pool of my own sweat. That, combined with everything else, has turned sleep into a luxury. In its place is this constant burden, which is continuously weighing down on me.

When I had started this job, I would have given anything to get rid of the nightmares that made me relive Angela's death over and over again. Maybe God really does have a sense of humor. Because if the nightmares of Angela were Hell, then these new ones are Hell's lowest level. But now, I've just about accepted them as a reality—just another part of the duty that must be carried out.

Hearing my lumpy phone start to go off, I quickly answer it and speak in my undercover character. "Sup?"

"Hey girl, it's Doc."

Yes, Doc is Marco's street name. "'Ey, man. Where you at?"

"I can't make it out to tha' spot. Can you meet me in my neighborhood?"

This is textbook. One of the cardinal rules of undercover work is that no matter what, you never change the spot of the meet after it's been set. "Change? What's wrong with 'dis place?"

"Can't make it."

"Why not?"

"I got places to be."

"So do I."

"I'm only five miles away, girl. Just come on over."

"I ain't goin. You comin' here or I'm taking my biz-niz elsewhere."

"Why you bein' like this? You a cop or somethin?"

Think fast, Ana. My tone suddenly changes. It becomes dark enough to scare any man or woman, even this punk. "Call me a cop and I'll reach through this phone and rip your throat out. Mah' brother's locked up."

"A'ight, a'ight! Sorry. Didn't mean to stir nothin'."

"So you comin' or what?"

"Yeah… I'm a comin'."

***

The deal with the so-called 'Doc' goes as planned and he will be busted in ten days. But for some reason, I don't feel accomplished. The thrill of every mission and case never dies. However, the fulfillment does. I guess that is what happens with anything. I think I learned something about that in an economics class my dad forced me to take. If memory serves me right, it is called the Law of Diminishing Returns.

As I arrive back at the station, the dispatcher—April—stops me in the hallway. Everyone here loves April. She is the stereotypical white, suburban, middle-aged lady, right down to her love for baking, and she is the mother we all wished we had. "Ana, your mom called… again."

Crap.

"I told her you were in a meeting," April continues.

"Oh, sorry about that. But thanks."

"She seemed a little concerned on the phone."

"I probably gave her reason to worry."

"Meaning?"

"I didn't go to church last week."

April's eyes slightly widen. "…why's that, hon?"

"…I feel off when I go there." I pause for a brief moment. "But thanks for letting me know. I'll call her back from my office."

"Good." She slightly smiles. "Because I'm running out of excuses as to why you're not available."

As I continue down the corridor, I cannot help but think of Mary. As close of partners as Bryan and I may be, it's not my business to meddle in his private affairs. I'm still not sure why I even went to the ball game in the first place. I felt nervous before and horrible after. And since then, I can't stop thinking about it.

But there was something… something in Mary's voice. She tried to sound harsh, but now that I think about it, it came out as more awkward than harsh. She's too nice to be rude. But in her voice, I sensed another element: loss.

Without even thinking, I turn around and start making my way toward the exit. Bryan would probably hate this. And yes, it really is none of my business. But in some twisted way, it is. If not for Bryan or Mary's sake, then for their son's.

***

Standing at the entrance of Mary's suburban home, I know this is my last chance to turn around. It's almost sunset. Even through the closed blinds, I notice that a few of the lamps inside are on. Someone is definitely home. But they haven't seen me yet. My heart is racing fast. I don't know if this is the fastest it's ever beaten, but it's defiantly going faster than any of the times when I was meeting drug dealers these past couple of weeks. I'd honestly rather be meeting ten of them right now than standing here. Oh, the irony.

Taking a deep breath, I muster my courage and ring the doorbell. I hear it echo inside the house. I take a small step back but keep my gaze focused on the heavy door. Sweat forms on my brow as Mary's harsh voice echoes through my head.

Please leave.

With those words fresh on my mind, I am disobeying them to the fullest. A few moments go by. I catch my foot quickly tapping against the pavement and stop it. The door stays closed. Maybe nobody's home?

My mind says that I've done my duty and should leave, but my heart says something else. Stepping up, I lightly press the doorbell once more. Again, I hear the sound echo through the residence. For a moment, I catch faint footsteps. They seem to be growing louder. I feel a gaze coming from the upstairs window, but when I look up, the closed blinds block my view. I focus back on the unmoved door. The situation has quickly gone from nervous to awkward.

I take a deep breath and let it out. I've done more than enough. It's time to leave. I try to turn and head back to my car. But against my will, my hand reaches out and rings the doorbell for a third time. I wince as I do and immediately begin to wordlessly berate myself, but I still wait to see what happens. Once again, my foot is quickly tapping against the concrete. I don't stop it this time. It doesn't matter anymore. My ears pick up some more footsteps. However, with each passing moment, they grow fainter.

Knowing what this means, I let out a sigh. I've made a fool of myself by coming here. A complete fool. Why do I do this to myself? Mary was right. It's none of my business. Bryan and I may be partners, but he's a grown man who knows what's best for himself and so does his wife. If I wasn't a cop, she probably would have called them on me. Damn my caring nature.

Burying my hands in my jeans' pockets, I do what I've wanted to do since arriving here and anticlimactically leave.

CHAPTER 11
VINNY THE RAT

The next morning is one of those rare ones where I don't wake up from a nightmare. Thank God for that. The peaceful, eight-hour sleep makes me the most pleasant person at the station this morning. It freaks some of my fellow officers out.

Not even a moment after I take a seat in my office chair, April follows me in. "Ana, you have a call on line three."

"Thanks."

"Did you get a chance to talk to your mom?"

"…no. Not yet."

I pick up the phone as April leaves and closes the door behind her. "This is Rocha."

"It's me."

Charlie. I recognize the man through his Clint Eastwood voice. From his words, you'd think he was in his sixties, but you'd be about thirty years too high. Charlie is my most reliable informant. He only ever calls when he has something good, and hearing his voice immediately excites me. "What have you got?"

"Something big. There's a dealer—actually he's a Lieutenant in Los Familia."

My eyes grow wide with surprise. "Lieutenant?"

"I know someone who is his loyal customer. This lieutenant has direct access to a den that supplies drugs to a good portion of Sugarland."

Is he serious? This is huge. I'm half surprised that I maintain my composure. "What's his name?"

"People call him Vinny the Rat, but I don't know his real name."

"That's good enough. Set up a meet with me and him."

"What do I say?"

I say the next words without missing a beat. "My name is Victoria Gomez. I've got access to some new areas in Pearland that include apartment complexes and businesses. I'm looking for a supplier. You and I met and you told me about his rep. I want him to be my liaison for the supplier. And I'm willing to give him a cut. A 15% cut."

There is a brief pause on the other end. *"...okay."*

"Tell him that when we meet, I'll have a contractor with me—he's the one giving me access to these areas." For this type of meet, it'll be best to have Bryan with me.

"That won't work. He will only agree to meet if you're alone."

"Can you at least give it a go?"

"Not without the risk of scaring him off."

I pause for a moment, my gaze focused on my desk. "...fine. Aim to set up the meet in the last spot we used. Let me know once you get something going."

"Will do."

***

I pull Vinny the Rat's file up from the archives. Standing under the dim lights and between the tall racks, I don't even bother taking it back to my office before opening it and flipping through the pages.

Victor M. Nelson, aka. Vinny the Rat
b. May 31, 1959
Height: 6'3" Weight: 230 lbs.

The picture we have is from his last arrest's mug shot two years ago in '97. He's a bald, light-skinned Hispanic with a long scar running down his right cheek. Probably got that from a nasty knife wound. From the headshot, I notice the strong muscles in his neck. Most of his 230 lbs seems to come from raw strength. He almost looks like a Hispanic version of Mike Tyson.

When he was arrested, it took three officers to bring him down and they all took their fair share of a beating from him. But what I notice most from the headshot are his russet eyes. They're the kind a seasoned brawler would possess: intimidating and fearless. They show that the man's fought for every inch he's gained in life. No doubt, he's not the kind of person you want to get in a fist-fight with.

He has quite the history: robbery, assault, illegal possession of weapons, and even murder. In his last trial two years ago, he pleaded guilty to all accounts. The only reason he's not on death row is because he escaped prison during a transfer last year. It was likely the work of his boss: Queen Bee—I mean Ebony Thorne.

There are several pages documenting the connection between Vinny and Ebony. As I read through it, my eyes light up, half from excitement and half from horror. I've come across plenty of Queen Bee's men. But they've only ever been the low-lying fruit who only know as much as they need to know about the gang. Even if they had the courage to speak out, they never knew anything that could help bring down their 'Queen'.

But this guy's something else. For a while, he was Queen Bee's personal hitman. He killed at least eight people in cold blood, presumably under her orders, but I wouldn't doubt that there are far more murders that were never uncovered. And the majority of his murders weren't simple hit missions. They were interrogations. Interrogations in which Vinny brought pain to his victims in every way possible before ending their lives. He cut them, burned them, electrocuted them, and beat them viciously. Vinny the Rat? More like Vinny the Devil.

However, he'll definitely know things—things that'll help put the Queen down. And now, he's going to get a load of me.

***

Bryan slowly looks through Vinny's file. He was already familiar with the name, just as every cop in this station is. I'm sure he's studied the file before. But he still takes his time, seemingly reading everything twice. Arriving at the end of it, he blankly stares at his desk for a long moment before looking up at me.

"Charlie told you about Vinny?"

I nod, still sitting across the desk from him.

"What's the plan, Ana?"

"Make contact with Vinny. Have him lead me to his supply house. I'll figure out the security details. I'm thinking it'll be a good hit: four dealers with a maximum of 10 kilos in storage. I'll lead a raid in two weeks. Get the drugs. Bust everyone inside—including Vinny. Case closed. Then we promise Vinny to keep him off death row if he leads us to Queen Bee and helps put her behind bars."

My partner takes a deep breath. "You may be getting ahead of yourself here. We need to think all this through one step at a time."

"The FBI and the force have been trying to bring Ebony down for years, but all anyone ever gets are the low-level street dealers. She makes sure they know nothing that could really hurt her. Vinny was her private hitman, and I bet he's still part of her inner circle. That's why she busted him out of prison to begin with: because he's important. This is a chance, Bryan."

"A dangerous chance."

"It'll always be dangerous going after somebody like Ebony. If it wasn't, she would already be locked away."

He leans forward a bit. "I'm not worried about Ebony right now. I'm afraid of you being with somebody like Vinny. He's a ruthless murderer, Ana. And you're a talented officer, but I've seen a lot of talented officers go out against people like him."

"I've seen the files—"

"But you weren't there to see the bodies of his victims. I was. I stood over those corpses. Hacked up. Mutilated. Tortured in every way possible. He's sadistic and insane, Ana. He's a vicious dog that doesn't think twice about killing."

"I've been dealing with dangerous people for months now."

"Not like this."

"I haven't lost yet, have I? The only other option is that we try and arrest Vinny on the spot. We can have SWAT lying in wait and they'll jump on him right when he gets there. But you and I both know that he'll smell it from a mile away and will never show up if we do that. This is the only way to make this happen."

There is a long, awkward silence between the two of us. Bryan keeps his eyes locked with mine, as if he's trying to stare me down. But knowing that he won't be able to change my mind, Bryan breaks the stillness. "What cover are you going to use?"

"Victoria Gomez."

He nods. "And the meet-up?"

"Charlie called me an hour ago. It'll be Friday afternoon at one."

"What's the set-up?"

"I'm meeting him. And…" This is the part I was dreading to tell Bryan. "…Vinny won't agree to the meet if anyone else comes, including Charlie."

Bryan raised his eyebrow. "You're going in alone?"

I slightly nod.

"No." He shakes his head. "It's too dangerous."

"Bryan—"

He holds his hand up to stop me. "Let me finish. The only way I'll let you go on this is if we do this my way. I wish you had told Charlie that I would be the one meeting Vinny, but what's done is done. Changing everything now will scare Vinny off and get Charlie killed. When you do make contact with Vinny, I'll be in the vicinity. Close enough to move in if anything happens but far enough to not be seen. For all we know, he might not be alone. Most likely, he won't be."

I wasn't expecting that reaction, and it throws me off for a moment. "Okay."

126

Bryan rises to his feet but keeps his gaze focused on me. "Listen, Ana. When this all goes down, if you get a hint—even the smallest hint that he's caught on, you draw your gun and bring him in even if it means blowing your cover."

I nod.

"This man's dangerous. He's a killer. Your life comes before the mission. Don't let your ambition cloud your judgment. No potential reward is the worth the risk of your death." He pauses. "And when you pull out your gun, make sure your finger is on the trigger… and don't be afraid to pull it if you have to."

"I won't."

After a brief pause, Bryan lightly nods. "Good. Let's go over the plan."

***

Vinny the Rat's eyes stare right at me, but they aren't looking at me through some photograph. No. These are in-person. And they're filled with cruelty, not displaying even an ounce of mercy as he aims a gun at my head from point-blank range.

The street is littered with corpses. Just like in every other nightmare I've had, the sky is dark and flames surround me. Buildings and cars are lit up, their thick smoke rising into the air. I feel their heat beat against my skin as my eyes remain locked with Vinny's brown pupils. I feel the muzzle of his pistol coldly pressing against my forehead but am unable to move.

This is a dream, but that knowledge doesn't do much for me. It does not lessen my trembling heart or ease my quivering. I'm completely immobile as I stare into Vinny's wicked gaze. Helpless, I watch as the edges of his lips form into a devilish smirk.

He pulls the trigger.

***

The day of the operation, I spend the morning hours in my office, filling out paperwork over different cases and going over the plan with Bryan once more. It'll be a normal meet. As long as I treat it as such, I'll be able to go through it without a hitch. I won't have my radio on me but will have my gun. Even if Vinny searches me before taking me to the stash-house, he won't be suspicious about me having a pistol since it's a common tool in my undercover character's line of work.

Cap agrees that this is a dangerous mission. Apparently, officers have gone after Vinny before but failed. One even died trying a little over a year ago. Cap would not have signed off on the mission, even if it meant losing Vinny, if it had not been for Bryan's backing.

Bryan plans to arrive at the scene an hour and a half before the meet. He'll find a nice hiding hole and make sure this is not a set-up. If it's not, then once I make contact with Vinny and am on my way to the stash-house, Bryan will tail us. If it is a set up on Vinny's part, we abort the whole operation and try to bring Vinny in the old-fashion way. I pray that's not the case because I doubt Vinny would even show up in that scenario.

Two hours before the meet, I pull back into my apartment's parking lot, needing to change out of my nicer clothes and into my undercover clothing. I quickly make my way up the flight of steps leading to my apartment door. Quickly unlocking it, I swing the door open and escape the heat by stepping inside. But I suddenly stop in my tracks.

Sitting on my couch is the last person I was thinking of seeing today.

"Mama!" For a moment, I think I'm dreaming before I remember having given her an extra set of keys to my apartment. I barely stop myself from instinctively drawing out my concealed handgun.

"Hey, Ana. Are you back for lunch?"

"Uh—yeah, yeah." *C'mon, Ana, compose yourself.* Thank God I'm not wearing my badge right now. "What's up?"

Mama frowns. "*What's up?* Is that any way to talk to your mother?"

Crap. Why the heck did I just say that? Horrible start. "Sorry, mama. Just slipped out."

"It's okay." She gestures for me to take a seat next to her on the long sofa. She's dressed in a loose brown tunic and a pair of white Capri pants, appearing as calm as ever. "I'm sorry for barging in like this unexpectedly."

"You're welcome anytime." I hide the lie well as always and take my seat. But I keep a couple of feet of distance between us. Please don't be here for the reason I think you are, and please don't do what I think you're going to.

"We need to talk, Ana."

I knew she would say that. I just knew it. And I also know exactly what it is she wants to talk about. Of all the times this could happen, this is undoubtedly the worst. "What's the matter?"

"I was concerned. You hadn't called me back yet. I've left at least ten messages between your home and office's phone."

"Sorry about that. I've just been busy with things lately."

"Listen, Ana, we're worried about you—all of us are. It seems like you've dropped off the face of the earth."

"I have a job now, mom—"

"A job—especially the kind you have—is only supposed to take up forty hours of your week, not your whole life."

She's about to go on a rant. I know it. And there's no stopping her when she does. Bad timing, mama. Seriously bad timing. "Mom, it's just been—"

"And it definitely should not be keeping you away from church, Ana, or even forcing you to leave early week after week."

Please, mom, don't lecture me now. Don't make me do this to you.

"I raised you with values, Ana. And I won't stand by and watch you throw them out the window right after you've got your freedom.

129

What did I always say: God, family, and *then* occupation. You've got that completely twisted right now."

I can't take this. I'm about to go and meet one of Houston's most notorious escaped prisoners and my mom is trying to lecture me. She needs to go. Now. And I need to get her to leave by any means necessary.

"I don't suppose you are even planning on coming to tomorrow's annual family picnic, are you, Ana? Is your job or whatever you're doing really more important than your family? Is that the kind of child I raised?"

No, I'm actually not planning on going. But it's time to end this. Every moment I waste here is a moment less to prepare for the meet.

"Maybe you shouldn't have a job like this if you're not ready for the responsibility."

Sorry, mama. "For God's sake, mom, can you please stop it!"

My voice shakes the room and nearly causes the flower vase to tremble. She suddenly jumps back an inch as my words sound off through the entire apartment. Her eyes are wide with shock as she hears me raise my voice at her for the first time in my life.

"I'm not a child anymore! You can't keep me pressed down under your thumb forever." My heart quivers with each syllable I utter, but I don't show it. I can't show it. Not now. "Maybe instead of me, you should have kept Angela like this. Maybe then, she would have never been volunteering in that soup kitchen to begin with. Maybe then, my sister would still be alive!"

The entire room falls silent. Deadly silent. *What did I just do? Did I really yell those words at her? I can't believe it.* I watch as tears suddenly swell behind my mother's eyes. But she keeps them from rolling down her cheeks. For an instant, I think that she's about to slap me. Or at the very least, yell right back at me.

But she doesn't.

In her eyes, I see something. Something that I have not seen since my sister's death. Something that I wished to never have caused my mother: pain. True pain.

She slowly rises to her feet before turning around. Without a word or another glance, she walks toward the door. As she does, she drops her key to my apartment on the floor before leaving. The door slams shut behind her.

As soon as she's gone, my head falls into my hands. *What is wrong with you, Ana? How could you say those words to your mom? Don't you know what you just put her through?* My heart shivers under the heavy weight that is suddenly crushing it. A flood of tears unexpectedly begins streaming down my cheeks as my body uncontrollably shakes. And all I can see in my mind's eye is the pain consuming my mother's eyes. I feel sick from my skin to the core of my soul, as if I'm rotting on the inside.

If there was ever a moment I have felt like committing suicide, this is it.

Stupid. Stupid. Stupid. People who do this—people who say things to their parents like I just said to my mom are the kind of people that burn in Hell. Those are the kinds of people that deserve nothing but misery and pain... and I've become one of them.

What did I just do?

CHAPTER 12
ONE SHOT

Unlike every other dealer I've met, Vinny the Rat shows up on time. It almost throws me off. I'm sitting in my parked car in the deserted lot when his dirty golden Lexus pulls up exactly at the strike of two. Driving his car straight at my Dodge Avenger, it's as if he's aiming for a head-on collision. But I don't budge, and his Lexus arrives at a screeching halt only a few feet away from my car's hood.

Jaw clenched, I push the image of my mama's pain-filled eyes out of my mind. This is really happening. It's not a dream or a nightmare. It's life.

There is a long and awkward moment as the two of us don't move. I stare into his eyes through the two windshields as he looks back with one hand hidden and one on the steering wheel. He hasn't even tried to disguise himself since his prison break. He looks exactly like his mug shot, even down to his shaved head. But the look of his brown eyes—that merciless gaze of his—is a hundred times worse in person than it was in my dreams.

He can't see, but my foot is anxiously tapping on the floor while my face remains expressionless. If I didn't have such good self-control, I would be hyperventilating. With my best effort, I block out everything else. I stop my nervous foot. Right now, I'm not Ana Rocha. I'm somebody else entirely. I'm Victoria. I'm a dealer who is here for business and is packing a concealed Glock.

Maintain control. No matter what, you are in charge here and you're the one calling the shots. Keep the mental edge and he's yours.

Vinny keeps a stoic expression as he searches for any hint on my face. No doubt, his concealed hand is holding a gun right now. He's sizing me up. I keep both my hands on my steering wheel, trying to indicate that I'm no danger to him. I know he won't hesitate to shoot me right here and now before we've even spoken a word if he suspects anything. What he's doing right now is making sure I understand that.

But he's not the only one here who's a threat.

He slowly gets out of his car but keeps his eyes on me. Underneath his rugged jeans and fitted shirt, he's a well-built man. It's easy to see how it would have taken three officers to bring him down. Even though he has at least twenty years on me, he's strong enough to strike fear into the heart of any man.

No mistakes, Ana. You can't afford those today. Let's do this.

I exit my Avenger and we close our doors almost simultaneously, neither one breaking gaze from the other. The air around us is about to crack. The hot sun beats down on me. But most of my sweat isn't because of the heat. I don't show any fear and I maintain full control of my expressions and body, making me radiate with poise. But my heart is racing as adrenaline pumps through my veins.

"You got a gun?" His voice is just like I imagined: powerful, cold, and calculating. It's not full of slang like all the other dealers I've come across. It's refined in its own way, reminiscent of a high-class criminal.

I slightly nod.

"Get rid of it."

My gaze still aimed at his face, I reach back and produce my Glock in a non-threatening way. I masterfully pop out the clip before slowly placing it and the pistol on the top of my car. I keep our eyes locked the whole time.

Vinny doesn't grow any less suspicious, keeping his hand close to his concealed weapon. "Charlie says you're serious news."

"I am."

"Your name's Vanessa?"

Nice try there. "Victoria."

"And why the hell should I work with you?"

"You already know that."

"I want to hear it from you."

I know why. He wants to see if I'm lying. Too bad for him, I'm an expert at that now. Mama became a victim of that not even—crap. Don't think about that right now, Ana. "Because I'll make you rich— much richer than you are now. You and your 'queen'."

He stays silent.

"We all know Pearland is going to boom in the next ten years. I've already got the things in place to get first dibs on a lot of the property. And if you work with me, my places are your places. I'll supply the customers. You supply the goods. Five years from now, you'll have tens of thousands of new customers. *Tens of thousands.* How much will your queen reward you for that?"

If my words have any effect on him, he's not showing it. He's got a good poker face. Silence falls over the two of us, each moment only adding another layer to the suspense. Finally, he replies. "If you're so serious, then how come you're new news to me?"

"Just got here from Dallas. Worked as a middleman for the Blue Ox. But then I got talking to Ant and—"

"Who?"

"Antonio Juarez. Arms dealer in Cypress."

"Never heard of him," Vinny replies.

"Then you're not in the right circles."

"I know *all* the right circles."

Liar. There's a long silence as he glares right at my face. *I know what you're trying, punk. And you can't read me. I won't let you.*

His voice changes. It becomes sadistic—the kind of tone you would expect from a torturer like him. "If you're screwing with me, I'll gut you like a pig right here." He takes a small step closer to me. "And if you're a cop… then by the time I'm done with you, you'll be cursing your mother for bringing you into this world."

Don't back down, Ana. Show him who is in charge here.

I step up as well, leaving only a few feet between us. I can smell his breath from here. "If I was here to arrest or kill your ass, you'd

134

already be down for the count. But I'm here for business. My boy Ant got me in touch with your boy Charlie. Charlie says you're a serious man. Said you were smart enough to jump on a good deal when you saw one. But maybe he was talking about somebody else, and maybe I should be talking to some other lieutenant of Queen Bee's. Because the *male* I'm staring at right now looks too stupid to know a good thing if it hit him in the face."

I pause for a moment before continuing.

"I think I know why you're no longer her favorite. There was a time she took you everywhere, but now you're nothing more than a has-been—nothing more than some punk whose best days are behind him. And this—this might be your best shot at redemption."

Standing this close to him, I finally realize just how big this man is. He could crush a person's skull with just one of his bare hands. But I don't let his size faze me one bit. Size is the last thing that matters in a standoff.

"So what'll it be, Vinny *the Rat?*"

Just as those words leave my mouth, fear suddenly grips my heart. I've pushed him too far. This is it—this is it. He's about to draw his gun or come at me right here and now.

No… no, he's not. He doesn't do a thing except briefly glance away for the first time. Did I get him?

He finally breaks the silence. "What do you want?"

Bingo. "Your stash house. I want to see it."

"We don't do that on the first meeting."

"You do when the score is as big as we're talking about."

"We have our ways."

"Listen. Before we talk about anything else, I need to make sure that your product is as good as people claim. Either we go to the stash house or this deal is over."

There's a quick flash in his eyes. Now I've pushed him too far. I was stupid for thinking he'd go along with this. He's too smart. It's all about to go to hell.

No... wait. He's going for it. Vinny takes a slow step back, showing no signs of aggression. "Get in my car. Leave your gun."

I'm in.

***

Holy—what am I doing? This has to be a dream. It has to...

I'm in the car with Vinny the Rat. I'm sitting next to a cold-blooded murderer who should be on death row. I've been matching him move-for-move in this mental chess game so far. A year ago, this would have been a nightmare. Now, it's reality.

But this is not the time for rejoicing. This mission just went from dangerous to deadly. At these close quarters, he holds almost every advantage if things go south. It'll be all about strength, and he has the edge in that by far.

Closing the door I keep my head facing forward but watch his every move. Does it really smell so fresh in here? The whole vehicle is impeccable. Definitely not what I imagined it would be. *Stay focused, Ana.* I don't wear my seatbelt—it'll only limit my movements. He does the same, but that's normal for any dealer. He switches on the ignition and the car turns on smoothly. He keeps his closer hand on the wheel while the further one stays at his side.

I try to maintain the confidence in my voice. "Where's the stash house?"

"You'll see."

The car backs up before turning to head toward the parking lot's exit. It travels somewhat quickly across the uneven gravel. No matter how badly my mind wants me to look at Vinny to watch for any hint of ill-intentions, I only observe him through my peripheral vision. I've come too far to screw up now.

Breath, Ana. Stay calm. You've got this punk. What does mama always say? Dang it, Ana! Don't think about that right now.

Is Bryan seeing all this? I'm sure if it was a set-up, he would know by now and have intervened. What—what if he was taken out by one of Vinny's men? No... no, Bryan's too good for that. Just breathe, stay calm, and—

All my thoughts abruptly disappear.

I suddenly lurch forward as the car screeches to a sudden halt. I barely stop my head from violently hitting the dashboard. My heart stops as I realize Vinny's foot is slamming down on the brake. And in the next instant, something is coming for me. A knife. Vinny's knife. I can't think fast enough, but my instincts take over. I instantly move as far as I can from him. My back presses against the side door. His blade drives straight for my throat. For a moment, I see my death. But when the knife's blade is only an inch away, my open palm smashes into his wrist, diverting the knife from tearing open my trachea. Instead, it plunges into the seat.

His opposite fist powerfully slams into my face. The back of my skull violently crashes against the window, leaving a crack. For a moment, I can't think or see. The hair on the back of my head grows wet. A small stream of blood pours out of the back of my skull. And when my vision and senses return, Vinny's open palm is pressed against my face. It's crushing my skull. He's suffocating me as the back of my head stays pinned against the window. My eyes are wide. Through the crack between his fingers, I see his free hand pull his knife out from the seat.

I—I can't breathe! My movements grow desperate. I try to knock his hand away. It does nothing. I try to break free of his grasp. I can't. He's killing me! God, he's killing me!

With all my strength, I can't escape. I can't get any relief. He crushes down on my skull harder with every passing moment. It starts to go black. I start to lose my vision for the final time. Is this what dying feels like? Is this what Angela felt? I can't breathe... I can't... I...

No, Ana!

You won't die here! Not like this to some murderous punk! Victoria might, but not Ana Rocha.

137

My free hand grabs hold of my second concealed pistol from the back of my jeans. Without hesitating, I reveal it. I don't think—I can't afford to.

Vision's almost gone black. Body is numb. I can barely see—barely move. The gun's barrel aims at Vinny's chest from almost at point-blank range. The bullet will tear through his insides like a spear. And as he sees it, he sends his knife down at me. But I sense something in him—something I never imagined Vinny the Rat was capable of: fear.

I pull the trigger.

CHAPTER 13
ONE LIFE

What happened? Last thing I remember, my gun's deafening roar is blasting in my ears. It's ringing through my head. And then my stomach is on fire. Something violently cuts through my insides. But now—in seemingly the next moment—I'm somewhere else completely. A police station... at least, that's what it feels like. The light burns my eyes and everything's so bright.

A shadow is standing over me. No... there are two people. Maybe three. Why is this light so bright? My head is throbbing and my brain feels ready to pop out of my skull. But at the same time, I feel so light-headed that I think I'm about to slip back into unconsciousness at any moment. My guts are sore and in pain—more pain than any cramp or stomach virus ever gave them.

"She's waking up."

The voice sounds familiar. But I can't get my eyes focused on anything right now. And I can hardly even think. It almost feels like a dream, but it's too real to be one. It's all too much. One thing for sure: that's not Vinny's voice. Thank God.

Even though I can't see a thing, my left hand travels down to my waist. Something there—just to the left of my stomach—doesn't feel right. It feels lumpy and unnatural. And right when my hand reaches it, I know what it is: stitches. Vinny got me good.

"Is she alright?" That's... that's Bryan's voice.

"She'll live. Just a long day is all... just a long day."

You can say that again.

***

"How are you feeling?"

When the heck did I wake up? After blacking out again, the next thing I know is that I'm sitting on a medical table in an unfamiliar room. I look straight ahead at a man dressed in a white coat. This isn't a hospital. Instead, it looks like the insides of a police station—a large one at that. The ceiling lights above me are lit and the window blinds are open, letting in the sun's rays. The white-coated man stares at me. I'm not sure if he's evaluating me or just waiting for me to speak.

"...well, I'm alive."

"That you are, officer."

I look down at my stitches. It's so dang sore. It feels worse than any beating I ever took in martial arts. I can't tell if that's from the stitching or the knife wound, but I would guess it's the latter. I've been changed out of my clothes and into a fresh pair of light brown capris and a modest, cobalt tunic.

"You took a couple of nasty blows, and you were in total shock when you got here. Cut on the back of your head. Your nose was almost broken. And worst of all was your stomach's knife wound. A few inches deeper and you may have very well bled out. But that partner of yours really knew what he was doing."

My gaze rises back to the doctor. "What happened?"

"After the—well incident—he pulled you out of the vehicle. He stopped the bleeding from your head, slowed down the bleeding from the knife wound, and got you here. I did the rest."

"...thank you."

He politely nods.

I try to shift positions, but wince when I realize how much it hurts to move. I almost ask what happened to Vinny, but stop myself. I already know the answer to that. I pulled the trigger. His black heart may very well still be sprayed all over the driver's seat of his car.

"Are you okay?"

I snap back to reality and dismiss the image of a dead Vinny. "Where is he? Bryan?"

"I wasn't told. But he'll be back here soon." He pauses for a moment. "There's one more thing I'm supposed to tell you though. Your informant was found dead."

My eyes widen. "Charlie?"

The doctor nods. "Nobody knows if Vinny knew from the start or not as to who you were. If he did... well, then you're very lucky to be alive. I'm sorry to be the one to have to tell you this. Please don't blame yourself for what happened. And please don't blame yourself for having to pull the trigger. I'm sure there's nothing anybody could have done differently."

Don't blame myself? Who else is there to blame? He says something else, but I don't hear him. As the doctor turns to leave, the vision of Vinny the Rat clouds my mind once more. I see his eyes. His now dead eyes. And I remember my finger on the cold trigger. I remember that I've taken the life of another human being.

I've killed.

***

A few minutes after the doctor leaves, two uniformed officers enter the room. One is quite a bit larger than the other and there's at least a ten-year age difference between them. The duo could easily masquerade as Batman and Robin.

From seeing the files in their hands, I know why they're here. They both take a seat right across from me after closing the door behind them. The next few hours pass in me answering questions—many of them the same one just asked in a different way.

These men want to make sure they know everything that happened. If I'm ever called for questioning, they want to ensure that all my ducks are in a row and that there are no missing holes in my account. Reliving the entire ordeal is the last thing I want to do right now. But I go along with it. Batman and Robin switch off. One of them asks me about the events leading up to the operation and the operation itself, while the other one asks questions regarding the assault and—of course—Vinny's death. As I answer their seemingly endless questions, they record every word of it.

However, I can't look either of them in the eyes. They both seem understanding enough. Maybe they've been in my shoes before. Or maybe they can see what I'm going through. Either way, they let me take my time and don't try to push me too far. Whenever the one asking questions about the fight feels like he's making me think back on it too much, he passes the reins back to his counterpart. It's nearly six in the evening by the time their questioning is finished.

After the Dynamic Duo leaves, I'm left with a stack of paperwork that needs to be filled out. I'm allowed to use one of the station's empty offices to do it. My guts aren't hurting as bad when I make my way there, but they're still ridiculously sore. I doubt that'll be going away any time soon.

The paperwork for drawing your weapon is a nightmare. But the paperwork for discharging a shot—let alone killing a man—is hell.

I do it all. The documents ask for every single minute detail, and I comply. I basically have to write down what I just spent hours telling the two officers. But the more I write every single fact, down to the smell of Vinny's sweaty hand as it suffocated me, the more the scene replays in my head. I am back in the golden Lexus with Vinny the Rat. He's suffocating me without any mercy. I feel his hand crushing on my skull. I can't breathe and can barely think. All I can sense is the life that's slowly leaving me. I see the knife coming at me, intent on gutting me. He's going to kill me like he's murdered countless others.

The gun is in my hand again. I feel its cold trigger. In it, there is life and death. There is the power to take life or spare it. Aiming my gun at his heart, I chose to pull the trigger. I chose to become a killer.

And it's something that will haunt my nightmares for a long, long time.

142

***

It's a little past sunset when Bryan arrives. I'm waiting for him in the solitude of the spare office, next to the stack of half-completed paperwork. I couldn't bring myself to finish it without risking a complete breakdown. Since the debriefing, nobody has bothered me except for a nice lady who brought me some food and water. I'm exhausted, but doubt that I'll be getting any sleep tonight.

Bryan wears a pair of blue jeans and a black, collared shirt. His badge and gun hang from his belt. There are a few dirt stains on it though. They're definitely from today. He warmly smiles when he walks into the office. "How are you feeling, trooper?"

I don't say a word.

He takes a seat across from me. "You've been cleared from what I hear. And I hear you remember everything too."

I slowly nod but remain silent.

His smirk disappears. "You okay, Ana?"

"… I… I killed him. I killed a man."

"Hey, look at me, Ana."

I do.

"You did what you needed to do. Nothing more."

"I've lied, cheated, shook hands with devils, and now I've killed. What is there left to do? What other sin is there?"

Bryan is silent for a long moment. "If you're worried about what God might be saying, I would guess that he understands. And if He doesn't, then He is not really God and you have nothing to fear."

"But now I have blood on my hands."

"Only the same blood a soldier has. Killing for pleasure or greed is a sin. Not in battle… or self-defense. It was your only option and you made the right call. If any authority in this state wants to challenge you on that, they'll have to answer to me."

A part of me wants to ask Bryan if he ever had to pull the trigger, but I don't. I notice a bit of blood on Bryan's clothing that goes along with the stains. It's fresh, not even a few hours old. He follows my gaze before looking back at me.

"Is that mine?"

He slightly nods.

"They told me you saved my life. Between my head and stab wound, I would have bled out if you weren't there."

"That's what partners do. They look out for each other. Nothing to it." Bryan pauses. "I'm not planning on losing any more partners. One is enough."

I try to smile, but can't. "Thank you."

He slightly smirks for half a moment.

"When you got there, was Vinny already…"

Bryan again nods.

"Before the operation… I did something. Something that made me deserve what I got. In fact, I got off easy." I take a deep breath as I look away. "My mom was at my apartment when I went home. She wanted to talk to me, but all I could think about was the mission. And—and…"

He patiently listens.

"What I said to my mom—the—the horrible things I said to get her to leave my apartment. The way I hurt her." Tears swell in my eyes. "It—I was a monster, Bryan."

I never told Bryan what happened, but he can read it in my eyes. And his gaze shows that he understands. "Now you know what happened to Jack… as well as me. You know that in time, the line between your two lives gets lost and one has to take over. We carry a burden—all of us. And it's one that we can never share with anybody."

"Is there any way to stop this all from happening? Any way I can keep that line alive?"

He lightly shakes his head as he glances at my feet. "I don't know, Ana. Maybe it can. Or maybe it's just a fool's dream."

144

There's more silence between us as his words echo in my head. The room grows uneasy as I don't know what to say. My mind is everywhere and has a thousand thoughts at its forefront: the trigger, mama's face, Vinny's killer eyes, and so much more. But Bryan's next words make them all disappear.

"We found the stash house, Ana."

I'm pulled back into reality. My eyes lock with his. What did he just say? After several moments, I bring myself to reply. "...how?"

"By the time you were being stitched up, I had a warrant to search through Vinny's car. He had a pager and a number repeatedly called him while we were searching. It was the landline for a small warehouse. But, interestingly enough, that warehouse was supposedly unused. Legally, the warehouse doesn't have an owner. The landlord died three years ago with no next of kin to inherit the land so the city took it. But three hours later, I was leading a raid on it backed by an army of SWAT."

Is this really happening? "How big was it—the stash house I mean?"

"It was the jackpot, Ana. Biggest I've seen in a while." Bryan lightly smiles. "There were six dealers there. We took them all down before they even had the chance to fire a shot. The whole bust took less than ten minutes. A little over fifteen kilos of cocaine were confiscated as well as several thousand dollars in cash. As soon as the raid ended, a seventh dealer—Percy Davies—was coming back from a drop-off. He tried to run when he saw us, but we got him too. We've been looking for him for some time now."

I'm silent. Completely speechless. I had known that whatever stash house Vinny would lead us to would be big, but this is amazing. I was thinking four dealers and eight kilos tops. I can hardly believe Bryan's words.

"All seven dealers are locked up. We've got one of the best interrogators in HPD working them. I'm sure within a couple of days they'll know that they're not important enough for Queen Bee to bail out and definitely not important enough to have a defense hired for them.

That'll make them more than willing to talk." Bryan pauses for a long moment, his grin disappearing. I sense the hesitation in his next words. "And there was something else you should know. Apparently, somebody had done one of the dealers wrong. And in retribution, they had kidnapped his sister earlier this morning and were going to sell her off. We found her in the attic, completely unharmed. I imagine that would not have been the case by tomorrow morning."

...what? Those—those animals. How... how could they even think of—

Bryan's words cut right into my heart as I imagine the fear the girl experienced and the vile minds of her captors. I tear my gaze away from Bryan and look down at the floor. They would have destroyed that girl's life. And all for just a grudge.

"Her name is Angelica."

Did I hear him right? Angelica? I slowly bring myself to look back at Bryan. For a long moment, everything else withdraws to the crevices of my mind. And where the visions of Vinny were, something else takes their place. "...Angelica?"

He simply nods. "Your operation saved her life, Ana. She has a younger sister—Ellie. And I know that Ellie will be grateful for you putting your life on the line."

This is too much. As Bryan's words echo in my head, all I can see is my own sister's face. All I can see is Angela's caring gaze. Shutting my eyes, I barely stop the tears from rolling down my cheeks.

"You can catch her in the hallway if you want."

***

Bryan leads me out of the office and into the brightly lit corridor. There are countless uniformed officers bustling through the hallway as they attend to their nightly duties. They don't pay us any heed. This station is much busier than ours. I realize that I haven't even asked anybody which station this is yet, but I'd guess we're somewhere in central Houston. The lock-up isn't too far from here and I hear some of the prisoners getting a little too rowdy. Entering the corridor, my legs are a little slow as I realize how utterly exhausted I am. I'm surprised I can even stand on my own.

"Captain Scott has given you a short leave of absence." My partner walks half a step in front of me but slow enough so that I can keep up. "I would really suggest you take the days off and a few more if you need them."

"I will."

"Please don't rush coming back to work, Ana. I'll page you if anything important happens with the interrogations."

Compared to our smaller station, this place is a metropolis. I've gone from the proverbial pond to ocean, leaving me as a fish out of water. There is so much going on around us that I can't keep up with it all. I'm not sure where my partner is leading me, but I slowly follow him without a word. We're definitely going the long way to the exit. Turning the corridor, we come to a much smaller and emptier one. But looking toward the far side of the hallway, I realize why Bryan has brought me here.

There's a girl, no older than eighteen, sitting on a bench. She has long, silk-like black hair. She's pretty, slender, and even from this far, I notice the innocence on her face. Her cheeks are wet with tears.

"That's Angelica," Bryan softly says.

Her mother, father, and older brother are all huddled around her. She's wrapped in their arms as they all cry tears of joy upon seeing her after what was the longest day in their lives. Just looking at them, I feel the warmth of their love.

But there is one thing that really gets my attention. Between the mother and father, hugging Angelica with all her strength is a little girl: Ellie. She's no older than seven—almost the same age I was when my sister was killed. With her eyes shut, Ellie is weeping and trembling uncontrollably. She has more tears flooding down her face than any other person there. In that single moment, I sense the bond between Ellie and

Angelica. I sense the selfless compassion. And above all, I sense their love.

We're too far to be noticed by them, but I wouldn't want to interrupt them anyways. My own dam bursts. Tears suddenly stream down my face, and I can't take my eyes off of the scene. In this moment, I can't feel any of my own ache. I don't see my mom's pain-filled eyes or Vinny's merciless ones. I forget that I was almost dead only hours ago. All those thoughts are flooded out by a light. Where Angelica sits, I am seeing something else. I'm seeing my own sister: Angela. And I see myself as Ellie. My own sister was taken from me... but Ellie's wasn't. Ellie will never have to go through the pain I endured.

And the fact that it was me carrying out my duty even in the face of death that made this possible makes me feel something I have not truly felt in years. Something that I thought was lost: joy. True joy.

"...thank you, Bryan." My heart is elated, and I don't tear my gaze from this precious sight. I want to take it in and remember every detail from this perfect moment.

I feel Bryan's hand lightly come onto my shoulder. "No, thank you. Thank you for reminding me of why we do this. It's not for us. It's for them. And a scene like this *is* worth putting our lives on the line."

CHAPTER 14
ANGELA

From the top of these hills, I can see everyone down below: mama, dad, Ramon, and Laura. I can even make out Laura's baby bump. And around them, I observe countless aunts, uncles, and cousins. It's the family's annual picnic and I'm the only one not there. There was a time when I looked forward to this event all year. But now, for the first time in my life, I'm watching it from afar.

It's the perfect weather for this sort of thing. There are enough clouds in the sky to beautify the heavens without becoming a nuisance. It's warm, but not hot. And a light, cool breeze only makes everything better. The younger people have several sports going on simultaneously while the older folk are just kicking back and talking the day away.

I can smell the mouthwatering food: enchiladas, tacos, fajitas, and even mama's famous chicken quesadillas. It's like a little Mexico down there. But I wouldn't expect anything less from a family reunion of mine, especially with my extended family there. Nearly half of them are professional cooks. They sizzle their food with so many spices and flavors that it nearly just melts in your mouth.

Watching the entire scene, my insides are in so much pain. Not even two days ago, I was almost dead. A man tried to stab me and strangle me to death in some deserted parking lot. He tried to murder me. And they will never know. They *can't* ever know.

Laughter faintly reaches me. There is so much happiness down there. Even from up here, I can sense the joy. In years past, I was a part of this jubilant life. I was as happy as they were. But today, hearing their joy only dampens my heart.

I have put a curse on myself. I chose to put on this uniform. I took the mantle of the badge. I made an oath to protect. If I had fully known what all it really entailed, a part of me wonders if I would have gone through with it? But deep down, I know the answer to that. It is undoubtedly a 'yes'. Even if I had never put on the uniform, I still would never truly be one of them. My laughter would never be the same as my family's. My heart would never truly be happy. All that disappeared the day Angela was killed. It was in that moment, when I stood on the top of those steps and heard my mother weeping, that I put on the uniform.

This is the only path for me.

Now I know what this all means. I know what happened to Bryan and Jack. It's happening to me too. That line between my two lives was once thick and clear. Then, it began to erode to a point where it was barely there. It happened so slowly that I never realized what was occurring until it was too late. And now... now I fear that the line is completely gone.

But Bryan...oh, God, Bryan has been living in the shadows for months—seeing nothing of his family outside of photographs. To see his family from so far without ever being able to touch them. He can witness their laughter, but never hears it or feels their warmth. He must live in the darkness so that others, like his wife and child, can bathe in the sunlight.

And even with all this—after these months and years—he has not lost his humanity. He has not lost his way. But how much longer can he last? I remember his voice the night he told me about Jack. There was something in it. It was a tone that told me he might not last much longer.

I know what I must do. Bryan saved my life... and I must save his.

***

I'm half surprised that Mary opens the door. And I'm even more surprised that she isn't holding a shotgun to scare me off of her front porch. My first thought is that she is going to immediately shut the door on me, but that theory quickly vanishes after she stares at me for a few moments.

Realizing that I've got a shot, I spit out my opening line before she has a chance for second thoughts. "I know I'm the last person you want to see right now, but if you just give me five minutes, I'll never bother you again."

After a long moment, she lets out a sigh. "Why don't you come inside?"

Please don't be dreaming, Ana. I follow her past the foyer and into the living room. It's a beautiful home on the inside. There's a feeling of warmth here. Hanging from the walls are aesthetic painting and pictures. I wonder if any of the paintings are Bryan's or Mary's? The home is well-lit and there's not a speck of dust anywhere. Mary definitely has an eye for this sort of thing. I plant myself in a recliner but lean forward a bit and Mary takes a seat across from me. There's a long, awkward silence before I break it.

"Where's Kevin?" Realizing how cold the A/C is, I start to regret wearing shorts here.

"At the neighbor's." She pauses. "I assume you're here for the same reason as last time."

I slightly nod. I notice a picture of Bryan on the table. "I know it's none of my business… and I don't want you to think that I'm here to bother you."

Mary is silent.

"…but Bryan's my friend. And I care about my friend's family. And even though you are separated, you're still his wife… at least legally." I hesitate. "But something tells me that you don't like this situation any more than he does."

She looks down for a quick moment. "This situation is complicated, Ana."

"I know it is. And I know he's hurt you before. But he's been hurting himself even worse every day… and you being gone has only made it worse."

Mary falls silent for a long time, obviously debating if she should tell me what she wants to. "…it was a year into Bryan's career when I noticed that there was a distance between us. I knew he was faithful to me. There was never any question about that. And I knew what his job was. I never was excited about the kind of job he had, but he was passionate about it and felt like he was making a difference, so I supported it. But even so, there was a rift. And the more time that passed, the wider it became."

I wordlessly listen on.

"I even met the people he worked with numerous times. But that didn't make a difference. He would wear this armor—I knew it was because of his duty. He would see things—bad things—that he didn't want me to know about. But a time came when he began wearing his armor at home. After Jack died… I tried to be there for him. I knew Jack's death put Bryan on the ropes, and I tried to help him out of it. But his armor was thicker than ever. The more I tried to help, the more he pushed me away. And the day I told him I was leaving… he didn't even try to stop me. He just got up and walked out of the house without another word."

There's another long silence. I know that if I was not here, there would be tears streaming down Mary's face after saying those words. I notice her holding them back behind her eyes.

I reach into my purse and produce a golden-framed photograph. "There's something you should see, Mary."

Mary takes it and looks down at the family photo that sits in Bryan's office.

"He keeps that at the forefront of his desk. He thinks I don't notice, but he looks at it every day. And whenever I catch him staring at the photo, I see something behind his eyes, Mary. Do you know what it is?"

She doesn't reply.

"Regret. It's regret. I know what kind of armor Bryan wears. He wore it around me when we first met, and I know how he can be distant. And I know he may not deserve another chance after the patience you've shown him." I lean forward a little more. "But maybe this duty has just made him forget how to show his emotions. Maybe it took the toll it takes on everyone else who wears the badge. Maybe it's taught him so much about putting on a show that he has forgotten that he doesn't have to wear his armor around you... but I don't think it's too late to remind him. And if you're willing to take a step toward him, something tells me that he will come running to you."

Mary glances down at her wedding ring as I continue.

"He loves you. He may not show it and there may be times when he doesn't act like it, but he does and he has never stopped. All I ask is that you give him another chance. Do that... and I promise nothing but good will come out of it."

After a long moment, her gaze comes back to me.

***

I don't have much time to digest what all occurred inside Mary's home. I went in there hesitant but left emotionally exhausted. I hope it was worth it. If she's willing to pick up the phone and call her hurting husband, then it will be.

The only thing I want to do right now is lay my head on my pillow and sleep the entire weekend away. Lord knows I need the rest. I can hardly even concentrate on the road right now. My soreness, emotions, and weariness make me feel like I just came out of a boxing match with Muhammad Ali and took the best beating he could give.

But even with all this, I don't know where to go. For some reason, I don't want to return to my apartment or go to the station. All I know is that I need to be somewhere where I can get my thoughts together and find some peace. I'm not even half a mile away from Mary's

153

house when my heart makes its decision. With everything that's happened, there's one place that I need to be. It's the only place where I can find solace no matter what is happening to me.

Without hesitating, I turn the car around.

***

There isn't anybody else in the graveyard today. But I don't mind. In fact, I like it when I have the place to myself; there's nobody here to disturb my conversations with my sister.

I take a seat on the ground a few feet from the tombstone. My gaze is focused on its engraving. The sun beats against my back and my shadow falls onto the base of the headstone.

The skies are clear and the sun is high up on this late summer day. But I hardly feel the heat. Just like every time I visit here, all I sense and all I feel is one thing: Angela's presence. I feel as if she's all around me, surrounding me, and smiling down with her loving gaze. I don't know if it's real or not. It's likely just my mind playing tricks on me, believing what it wants to believe. It wants peace so badly that it's willing to lie to itself just to feel a bit of comfort. But I don't give a damn if it's real or not. That doesn't matter. The only thing that matters is that when I'm here, I feel safe from everything else. I can forget what I lost all those years ago and forget what reality is. And for as long as possible—even if it is just a brief moment—I can be a younger sister again, confiding in my best friend.

With a sigh, I read the engraving on the tombstone—the name, the date, and the inscription—for the millionth and first time. Even after all these years, I can't comprehend seeing Angela's name on a tombstone. It continues to feel surreal. I've spent more years without her than with her, a thought hard enough to believe, but my heart and soul refuse to accept the fact that I'll never set eyes on her again.

It's been a while since I've been here. Too long. Perhaps that's why I feel so lost. I know now that rushing to meet Vinny the Rat was idiotic. I should have listened to Bryan and Cap. Instead, I was so consumed in my duty that I forgot about myself. It ended well and the life of another was saved through it all, but the outcome had nothing to do with me. It was all pure luck. If fortune had not been involved, I would be dead.

But perhaps worse than being dead, I now have blood on my hands… even if it was in self-defense. That is a weight that I will carry with me until the day I die.

However, coming here and sitting before my sister, I'm home again. Everything feels so right now that I'm isolated from the world. I look down at the bottom of the gravestone, continuing to feel Angela's presence.

Some people go to a priest to confess and speak their fears. My mother does and so does my father. But me? I come here. I confess to my sister. "I bet you never imagined seeing me like this… all beaten up and doing the things that I do. But then again, I bet you never imagined me buying drugs for a living either."

The tombstone remains silent. I take a long moment to study it. It's been weathered down by the years. When we lowered Angela into this grave over a decade ago, the headstone was smooth—as smooth as they come. But now it's rigid and coarse. There are several small cracks along its surface. It's lost its innocence, just as I have. The more I've delved into the shadows, the more it has worn down.

"I've done everything I said I would when I came here all those months ago… even killed." I say the last words so softly that I barely hear them. "I wish there had been another way. And God, it'll haunt me forever. But to know that by almost dying, a girl was saved and reunited with her family, it makes it all worth it. To know that another sister will not go through what I did makes me know that something good came out of it. I hope that God sees that as well, and I pray you do, too."

There is a pause.

"I hope you're not looking down at me, disappointed in what I've become—disappointed in what I've done. I've tried everything else to find a purpose for what happened to you. But all I found were unanswered questions. But here—here I can justify what happened to you. I can say that your death led to countless good things: all the criminals off the streets and all the lives that have been saved. I would give it all up if it brought you back... but I can't."

As I speak, I hear Bryan's words echo in my head: *we can't bring back the dead.*

"All I can do is keep moving and make your sacrifice worth something. And this is the best way—the only way—I know how, Angela. It's... it's the best way I can make sure what happened to me won't happen to anyone else." I take a deep breath and let it out, calming myself. "It's the only way I can take all the unanswered questions and sorrow that I was left with and try to make something good come out of—"

Beep!

I instinctively jump back. My thoughts abruptly disappear when my pager suddenly goes off. After being thrown off for a moment, I snatch the device off of my belt. As expected, it's Bryan who's trying to get in touch with me. And it can only mean one thing: there's been a breakthrough with the interrogations.

Without hesitating, I rise to my feet and leave.

***

"Thank you for coming, Ana."

"What's going on?"

Bryan is waiting for me right outside the chamber that leads to the interrogation room. And right next to him is another officer—Joel Rivers. Based on Joel's reputation with questioning, I assume he must be leading up the interrogations.

Besides the three of us, the corridor is nearly empty. There are a few other personnel meandering further down the hallway, but they are well out of earshot.

"Are you feeling okay?" Bryan asks.

I nod before repeating myself. "Any breakthroughs on the interrogation?"

"We got them all."

"They all confessed?" The words fire off and my eyes widen in excitement. But even as they do, I can see that there's something in Bryan's gaze. He should be happy that they all gave in so quickly— anybody else would. But instead, where there should be a sense of accomplishment, there is a look of hesitancy.

Bryan nods as Joel speaks with a slight smile. "This must be some kind of national record. One of us may be getting a promotion from all this."

"Did any of them talk about Quee—Ebony?" I quickly ask.

My partner shakes his head. "They didn't bend on that end— none of them."

"They're definitely scared of something," Joel adds.

"Are you going to push them more?"

"They aren't going to say anything that can link Ebony Thorne as the head of *Los Familia*," Bryan answers. "They probably don't know anything that could. Everything that they've told us about the organization itself is nothing that we didn't already know."

"Except—"

Joel hardly says the word before Bryan cuts him off. "Why don't you give us some privacy, Joel?"

With a quick nod of understanding, Joel goes to the far side of the corridor, leaving the two of us alone. I watch him leave without a second glance. What was all that about?

"Ana..." Bryan looks down at his feet for a quick second. "There's one thing that we learned and it's something you should know."

"Shoot." Is this what he was hesitant about earlier?

"Six of the perpetrators that confessed are in the lock-up. But the seventh—Cedric Wilson—is still in the interrogation room. He already confessed to a couple of recent murders and will get a minimum of life in prison. But that's not why we are still working him. He said something." Bryan awkwardly clears his throat. "And what he said concerns you. It's something that... that I think you should hear from me."

Cedric Wilson? Why does that name sound familiar? "Tell me."

"He claims to have been working for the same cartel—*Los Familia*—for eighteen years now. We know Ebony Thorne heads up the cartel, even though we and the FBI can't ever connect all of the evidence to prove it."

Where is this going? I stare at him intently—almost blankly. A hint of fear creeps into my eyes as I hear his tone. Why is he so afraid to speak right now?

"Fifteen years ago, he went to prison and he got out after a four-year stint. He had been locked up on the charges of murder, attempted murder, illegal possession of weapons, and destruction of property." Bryan pauses. "All these crimes occurred when he partook in the drive-by shooting of a soup kitchen. But since he was a minor, he was tried as such and couldn't be put on death row. Instead, he got off easy."

Wait... a soup kitchen? Is... is he saying—

"Two hours ago, during the interrogation, he claimed that the soup-kitchen shooting happened on the orders of his boss—the head of *Los Familia*. The... the sole person murdered during the shooting was—was..." Bryan pauses. His voice is shaking and he can hardly look me in the eyes. "Angela... Rocha."

The world stops.

My face is pale. Deathly pale. *Angela Rocha.* The name echoes through my head again and again and again. No... no. This can't be true. It can't.

"I'm sorry to be the one to tell you this, Ana. But you have the right to know... I would want to know."

Is this happening? I—I can't think. I can't comprehend any of this.

One of the punks responsible for killing Angela is in the same building as me. He's breathing the same air. He's seeing the same walls.

And the one who ordered the hit that caused Angela's death is Ebony Thorne. It's the woman that nobody can touch. No, this has to be some sort of twisted nightmare. Any minute now, I'll wake up and it'll all be over. This can't be true—it can't be...

But I don't wake up.

"That bastard!"

My blood-curled scream shakes the entire building. Bryan powerfully grabs me and stops me from breaking into the room that holds the killer. My hysteric voice echoes loudly through the empty corridor, startling every person in ear-shot. Bryan's large hand grips mine, keeping me from drawing out my gun. With all my strength, I try to break free to come face-to-face with the murderer, but he restrains me.

My eyes are wild. My voice is violent. Veins are popping out of my forehead. And my mind is only focused on one thing: to end Cedric's life—to put a bullet in that pig's head. But I cannot even take a step as Bryan tightly holds me.

"Let me go! Let me—!"

"Ana! Please. You need to calm down."

I don't. I can't hear him right now. If anything, I intensify. But no matter what, Bryan is too strong for me. He won't let me move a muscle as he holds me against my will.

"Please, Ana. You're better than this." His voice is shaking. It's as if he can feel my pain. "Don't do anything that you'll regret. Think clearly."

There are several other officers now in the corridor, staring at us. But they do nothing to intervene and simply watch the scene unfold with wide eyes.

My eyes are locked on the door between me and Cedric. "That— that pig is sitting there and—and he killed my sister!"

Bryan is silent but still restrains me.

"And you want me to let this go!?"

Adrenaline is pounding through my veins. I can feel it. And it gives me the strength to inch closer to the door. I slowly begin to break out of Bryan's grasp. But I suddenly feel Bryan's powerful arm come from behind me and wrap around my neck. He constricts it a little, sending the message.

"Don't make me do this, Ana."

I continue to move forward and he squeezes a little more, beginning to narrow my air passages.

"Please…"

I feel the oxygen leaving my head. But I don't relent.

"Ana!"

I don't know if it's his voice or actions, but my senses flood back in. As quickly as I started, I abruptly stop and my body relaxes. Bryan breathes a sigh of relief and lets me go. I immediately collapse to my knees, exhausted. However, my heart is on fire.

"Thank you, Ana."

After a few deep breaths, I raise my quivering gaze to meet his. My eyes are filled with a rage—no, not rage. It's a focused anger. "Ebony Thorne. I need her file. Now."

***

"Absolutely not."

Captain Scott stares at us from behind his desk. With his arms crossed, he keeps his gaze steadied on me while Bryan stands at my side. Hearing his stern words throws more fuel onto my already blazing fire. However, it's what I expected him to say. He likely heard about the scene I caused less than an hour ago.

"Sir," Bryan begins, "We need to see Ebony's file."

"No." Cap shakes his head. "Right now, Ana needs to be at home. More so now, given the situation we have."

"We may be missing something here, sir." Bryan won't let this go that easily. "With this last bust and all the evidence we have, all we need is one more good piece of evidence to link Ebony Thorne to *Los Familia*.

One piece to show that she's the mastermind behind the cartel that floods the streets with more drugs than any other gang."

"If we're going to bring Ebony down, we need something big, Bryan. You should know this already. One small piece of evidence won't be enough. We'd need nothing short of a damn confession. Nothing less will do and nothing less will keep her behind bars for very long. She's too well connected."

"But we have to start somewhere."

"We have started. We've been after her for a while. This goes higher up than me and a hell of a lot higher up than either of you." Cap pauses for a few moments. "HPD's Narcotics Division has tried everything and we're still trying. But Ebony's smart. Now the FBI has taken up the crackdown's ropes. They've had agents go—and remain— deep undercover in *Los Familia* and work up the ranks over several months. Now they've been able to authenticate what we've theorized for so long."

What? Is he serious? I knew the FBI was after her but I wasn't thinking to this extent.

Cap's gaze returns to me as if he hears my mental question. He uncrosses his arms. "Ebony Thorne owns numerous businesses throughout Houston and Greater Houston. Legal businesses. Restaurants, bars, hotels, car washes, auto shops, and nightclubs form the majority. There are 70 in all. We've believed for a long time that drug money is being laundered from the businesses—especially the nightclubs and restaurants. Boxes of alcohol, napkins, supplies, and just about anything are used as a front to conceal the drugs and money coming in and out of the businesses. The FBI is now claiming that each of these businesses can contain as many drugs as a large stash house at any given time."

"Why would the FBI be telling us this?" Bryan fires off. "They've never been one to share information with us. And we've searched these businesses before—"

Cap looks his way, cutting him off. "Because they are going to need our help."

"How?"

"It's always been hard to get warrants for Thorne's businesses. They've always been clean from a legal standpoint and we've had to reach to find probable cause to search them. But we never find anything because she always seems to know which business we're after."

"Does she have an inside man?"

"I wouldn't doubt it. Between all the officers, judges, and people involved, it wouldn't be hard for her to find one weak link. Whenever we try and bust one business, she probably just moves everything over to a different one." Cap briefly glances down at his desk before again focusing on me. "The FBI is about to run a sting operation—one of the largest any of us will ever see. And they're not just hitting one of Thorne's businesses. Not even two. They're going to raid *every single* one of Thorne's business simultaneously. All the restaurants, nightclubs, hotels, shops, car washes, and even her damn fruit stands—we're hitting them all in one sweep. And for this kind of operation, the FBI needs HPD's manpower."

No way. I hear every single one of Cap's words, but I can't believe them. An operation this huge? Is it even feasible?

"Holy—" Bryan barely stops himself from saying the next word. "When's it all going down?"

"Three days from now. It'll all go down at exactly one in the afternoon. With every business hit simultaneously, she'll have nowhere to hide her goods. And we're playing it tight to the chest. Right now, only the FBI, judges involved, and everyone my rank and higher know—outside of you two. The officers involved won't know until the morning of. Even if she finds out, she won't have any time to move the drugs."

"So how do you want us to prepare?" I finally ask.

Cap is slow to reply. "You, Ana? Nothing. Bryan will be assisting with the raids. We need every man we can get. But you—you'll be home until this all goes down. And you won't be back here until next week."

"Si—"

"That's an order, officer." After a long moment, Cap looks away. "Now get the hell out of my office."

CHAPTER 15
THE RAID

Minutes after Cap throws me out of his office, I'm leaving the station. I can't stay here anymore. My fists are clenched and my heart is racing. The whole place has become sickening. How can this all be happening? In one day, my entire world has been shattered. One of my sister's killers is in this wretched building. The fact that he'll be spending the next decades of his life in prison does not console me. After all, it won't be for killing my sister that he's locked away. He got off easy for that. And he will never see the pain that he caused my family.

But now I've discovered the mastermind behind all my family's suffering and the things I've seen over these last months... and I won't have a hand in putting an end to it all. I won't be there to bring down the woman responsible for my lost childhood.

When I'm a few feet from the exit, Bryan's hand lands onto my shoulder from seemingly nowhere. "Merry Christmas."

I whip around to arrive face-to-face with him. Seeing what's in his hands, I take the unmarked, brown folder before looking back up at him. The pages in there feel warm, as if they were freshly printed. Is this what I think it is?

"It pays when people owe you favors." He keeps his voice low enough so nobody else can hear us. Bryan gives me a quick wink before turning. "I hope you find what you're looking for."

He leaves without giving me a chance to thank him. I immediately head through the parking lot before arriving at my car. I don't even bother switching my vehicle on before I rip open the envelope and the copy of a file spills out.

Ebony Thorne
b. October 13, 1962
Height: 5'5" Weight: 140 lbs.

In all my months here, I have never seen her face. But now it's right in front of me. The photo isn't a mug shot. It's recent—only five-years-old according to the date on the bottom—and was taken without her knowing. I have heard and uttered her name so many times, but I never thought about what she might look like.

She has fiery, red hair. The photographer took the shot from afar, not wanting to be seen. She's turned at an angle, so I can only see the right side of her face. But even from seeing just one of her emerald eyes, I notice something in them: authority. She's standing outside her nightclub speaking to a couple of men dressed as bouncers and pointing at something. Studying the expressions of the two men, it's clear that they know who's in charge.

Underneath her leather jacket and pants, she possesses a relatively strong and stocky physique. She's half an inch shorter than me. According to the file, the photo was taken outside of her largest nightclub & restaurant: The Green Beetle Club. She can be seen there often and is in a relationship with the place's manager.

Putting the file into my dashboard, I start up my car and pull out of the lot.

***

The Green Beetle Club. Oddly named since it's not even a club, even though there is one—also owned by Ebony—just down the road called Desire. But as for the Green Beetle Club, the first two floors are a five-star restaurant while the third is a private meeting and dining room. I'm glad I changed into some of my more fancier clothes before coming here. Dressed in a knee-length flowery dress and a white bolero, I fit right in.

Soft piano music reverberates through the restaurant. It's played live by a well-dressed pianist on a raised stage. It's too early for dinner but too late for lunch right now, so the place is nearly empty. However, a man dressed in a white shirt and red vest greets me at the door.

"Good afternoon, ma'am."

"Hi." I give a quick, polite smile.

"For how many?"

"Just myself."

He leads me to a table not too far from the pianist, but far enough so that the music won't be right on top of me. The tables are all draped in white linen. Brightly lit chandeliers hang from the ceiling. As I arrive at my destination, the waiter pulls out the red leather seat for me. Last time I came to a place this fancy, mama and dad were still paying my bills.

"George will be with you shortly, ma'am. Can I offer you something to drink? Some wine, perhaps?"

"Just a Sprite would be nice."

"Yes, ma'am." With a slight nod, he leaves.

From a first glance, I estimate this place could probably seat at least 175 people between both floors. A beautiful spiral staircase draped in an elegant red carpet leads from the first to the second floor while another staircase leads to the third floor.

An opening allows a view into the kitchen. The chefs are dressed in the kind of attire you'd expect at a nice restaurant, and the kitchen seems spotless. I look around at the other patrons. There are about twenty in all. They're all dressed nicer than the average person off the street and seem to be here in groups of two or three. They remain engrossed in their own conversations and don't pay me any heed.

Out of seemingly nowhere, another handsome waiter—presumably George—places my drink in front of me along with a basket of assorted breads. God, that aroma is mouth-watering.

"Is this your first time here, ma'am?"

"Yes, it is."

The expected pleasantries continue between us like they would at any restaurant. I don't even pay much attention when I do order my appetizer—I think it may have been shrimp in lobster sauce. But that's not what I'm here for.

I'm here to see the enemy.

It doesn't take long. The file claimed that Ebony Thorne is seen here and at Desire more than anywhere else. She supposedly uses the meeting rooms on the top floors of each place for her high-level deals. For all I know, she could be up there right now. Of course, that's never been proven. Hearing something from behind me, I turn around.

The world stops.

My eyes widen. My heart freezes. It... it's her. I'm staring at her—at Ebony Thorne. I am looking at the one I came searching for.

She pushes through the front entrance. Her fiery red hair hangs freely, and she's dressed in a pair of dark blue jeans while a loose blouse covers her fair skin. She storms in and the host at the door doesn't dare say a word to her. In fact, it seems as if everybody ignores her, acting as if she's not there. Even from here, I notice several wrinkles on her face. I'd imagine that half are from age and half are from the memories of what she's done. But her eyes are fierce.

Is this really her? Is this monster truly just a woman? Behind her is a man no less than 6'5" and 250 pounds of pure muscle. He possesses a face similar to Vinny the Rat's. Not in the sense that he looks like a twin, but in the sense that he's a fighter too. He walks as if he owns the place, but it's obvious that he's just her loyal dog who follows her around, barking at anybody that gets too close.

The surreal feeling vanishes and is replaced by something else. Rage suddenly courses through my veins—the same rage that flooded me at the station. My vision tunnels onto her, blocking out everything else. My heart quivers and I feel my clenched fist start to quake.

If I hadn't left my gun in my car, I would have pulled it out and shot her.

Instead, I watch her make her way through the restaurant and toward the kitchen, her loyal henchman at her side. Why do I get the feeling she's not here just for fun? Her expression says that somebody here has a price to pay.

The kitchen doors swing open before a man dressed as the manager steps out with a smile on his face.

"Hey—"

Clap!

Before the manager finishes the word, he's picking himself up off the floor. Spitting out a bit of blood, one of his teeth seems to chip off. The man lets out a loud groan as he tries to get himself back together. He crawls onto all fours, but Ebony again kicks her boyfriend, knocking him back down.

A few of the guests turn and look at the scene, but many of them ignore the commotion. It's as if this whole thing is invisible to them. Holy crap, is this really happening?

"You ever pull a stunt like that, and I'll have Pedro rip your damn head off." She looks at Pedro and gives him a quick nod. The intimidating bodyguard steps up with a vile smile. Without seemingly much effort, he cocks his leg back and powerfully kicks the manager in the head, keeping him down.

The manager stays down this time. He lets out another long groan of pain. My first instinct is to get up and stop this. But I don't. Nobody else is acting strangely. Either they're affiliated with all this or they're regulars. Either way, if I pick a fight, I'll be fighting on her turf and her terms. Big mistake.

And so I sit and watch as Ebony turns and leaves her half-unconscious boyfriend on the floor. She pushes through the doors and walks out as if nothing happened. Pedro follows her out like a dog.

So this is the enemy.

***

The next days pass by slowly. It's almost like I'm trapped in some vortex where time is standing still. I spend the days aimlessly wandering around my apartment. I don't hear from Bryan, Cap, or anyone at the police station. Not much of a surprise there.

I try to keep my mind off everything. But all I can think about is the bust. This kind of setup is what every cop lives for. It's going to be the operation of the decade and I won't be a part of it. I try going for a run every morning, but can't get into it. I try switching on the television, but ever since taking on this job, TV shows don't exactly hold my attention for very long and the news only upsets me. To top it all off, I can barely sleep.

Crap, I hate this.

I'm literally isolated. My phone doesn't ring even once. Nobody comes to visit: no neighbors, no friends—actually, I probably don't have any real friends outside of Bryan—and, not surprisingly, no family. I've given up everything for this forsaken duty. I threw my chips in with this lot. But now the duty has abandoned me and I'm left with nothing. Maybe I deserve it. Maybe I deserve to experience the punishment of loneliness.

Every time I'm in my living room, all I can think about are the last words I said to my mom. I'm hardly eating one meal a day, and I'm not even sleeping three hours a night. I can't do anything—anything but live with a heavy heart and the feeling that I'm powerlessly letting sand slip from between my fingers.

My days are spent in the larger bedroom—the one that is completely bare, save for the web of facts that covers one wall. I spend hours of my days staring at the web. Angela's face is at the center of it all. I always knew that somebody had ordered a hit on that soup kitchen the night she was murdered. I had searched for a name for years but always came up empty. The largest thing written on the wall is a simple question:

WHO ORDERED IT?

Now I know. But that knowledge does not serve me any good.

As I sit there, staring at the wall, I relive the night she was killed countless times. Sometimes, my face is blank. Other times, I feel myself shaking with an uncontrollable rage. But many times, streams of tears flood my cheeks, and my sobbing consumes the entire apartment.

I don't want to go on. I can't breathe. Without Angela, I feel like I'm suffocating. I've never felt her loss as badly as right now. Maybe I've just been suppressing it all along. But now that I know the name of the shadowy figure I've searched for—now that I know the name and have seen the face of the villain behind everything—my entire world is crashing down on me.

By the end of this week, Ebony Thorne will either be behind bars or she will have made a fool of the entire FBI and Houston Police Department. I don't know how she can get away with it, even if she does somehow catch wind of the operation. And if they don't bust her on this, it will be nearly impossible to get any local judge to sign off on any search warrants for Ebony's businesses any time in the near future. Once again, she would get away with her crimes.

The woman responsible for Angela's death is on the ropes to being brought to justice. And even with my badge, even with my gun, even with my title and accomplishments, I can't do a damn thing.

This must be what helplessness feels like.

***

Thursday night finally arrives. The evening news starts with a breaking news report. It's the one I've been waiting for. The news anchor sits behind a desk as a large banner on the bottom of the screen reads: 'BREAKING NEWS: BUST GOES BAD'

My face suddenly turns white. The world stops. No… please no.

"Today, an unprecedented operation manned by Houston PD and led by the FBI searched over 75 businesses. The linking chain between these businesses is that they are all owned directly or indirectly by a native Houstonian, Ebony Thorne. The

police say they were under the belief that the businesses were a front for drug importation. However, nothing was found."

Without thinking, my fist slams against the armrest, sending a loud thud throughout the apartment that nearly shakes the walls. No! No! No!

"*Here's what Ms. Thorne had to say about the situation.*"

The scene switches from the news-room to outside one of Ebony's restaurants. I find myself staring into Ebony's eyes through the screen. A crowd of people surrounds her—many of them reporters—but she focuses on the camera as she speaks. Unlike in the restaurant, her voice is civilized and so are her eyes. She knows how to mask them as she wears a charming smile.

"*Well, I'm not sure what brought the FBI and police down on us, but I'm sure glad they didn't find anything. And, who knows? Maybe the publicity will help out!*"

The crowd around her lightly laughs.

I slowly rise to my feet, shaking in rage. The television goes back to the newsroom. But I don't hear a word. She got away. Again. The FBI went after her and they couldn't touch her. They couldn't do anything more than the police. Once again, she gets away scot-free. But this time, she made a laughing stock of everyone involved. Ebony Thorne... she can't be caught. She's untouchable. The snake is always one step ahead. And if anybody does get a hand on her, she just turns around and bites them.

Suddenly, my arms run in a wild fury and my fist collides with the wall. The thud echoes through the room. Then again. And again. Each strike is harder and faster than the last. "God! God! God!"

With each word, my hands slam into the wall as if the wall was Ebony Thorne herself. I let out all my anger. I don't care about the pain. I can't even feel it right now. My face is red and my eyes let out tears of anger and sorrow. Once again, a person responsible for Angela's death has gotten away. "God! God! God!"

And I was powerless to stop it.

***

My cheeks are wet with tears when the night is at its darkest. Ebony Thorne. Queen Bee. Those two names fill the confines of my mind down to each and every crevice. And as I hear the snake's names over and over and over again, all I can see is the face of my dead sister.

When she was stripped from me, I was a child and could not do a thing. But now, when her killer was so close to being brought to justice, she slipped through the law's fingers just like the shooters did. And once again—even as an adult—I couldn't do anything to stop her. Again, she was protected by the shadows.

My head bows lower with every passing moment. It's all over now. I've failed... I've failed... *I've failed.* I'm sorry, Angela. I'm sorry...

No!

I suddenly sit upright. The tears stop. And the sorrow disappears from my eyes. It's replaced by something else. One of my hands clenches into a tight fist as my body shakes with a rage that has never befallen me before. Angela's face is replaced with the eyes of the woman responsible for everything: Ebony Thorne.

The name Ebony means darkness. She thinks she rules the darkness and that it protects her. But she hasn't seen anything yet. She has not gotten a load of me. She has not gotten a load of Ana Rocha. I'm not afraid. I'm not sad. And I'm anything but helpless.

I'm angry.

***

Friday morning, I disobey Cap's orders and charge back into the station. There's no way I will wait until next week. I'll go mad if I do. I nearly went mad last night—madder than I've already become.

The place is in a frenzy, no doubt from yesterday's debacle. What is normally a calm place is loud and rancorous. Everybody seems up to

172

their necks in work, scurrying from one office to another. *Am I at the right place?*

A few steps into the building, Bryan spots me. And like I expect, he tries to get me to leave. "Ana!"

"Not now, Bryan."

"You—"

"*Not. Now.*" The look in my eyes makes him back off. "Where is he?"

"…in his office," Bryan replies.

Cap's door is closed but unlocked. A shut door always means go away, but not today. Through the closed blinds, I make out the shadow of a visitor. His loud, authoritative voice spills into the hallway and stops me from opening the door right away.

"She knew we were coming, Scott! As soon as your office—"

"My office!?" Cap fires back. "The Intel was yours and you're blaming my office!?"

"Not just your office—the whole HPD! The operation was airtight until you all got involved."

"Without our manpower, there wouldn't have even been a damn operation in the first place! And almost nobody knew until the day of—"

"Don't try to cloud the fact that Thorne's got people in HPD!" The stranger loudly replies. "She likely has at least one person in this building. But we haven't lost everything yet. If you let me talk to her, we may be able to salvage all this."

"No, absolutely not! Not after what—"

This is probably the worst time to walk into the office, but who gives a damn right now. I push open the door and go inside. As soon as I do, their voices suddenly cease and their gazes focus on me. Cap's face is reddening as he stands behind his desk with his open palms pressing onto it. He's covered in a bit of sweat. The other person—a dark-skinned man—is dressed in a suit and tie. He possesses a G-man look. Definitely FBI.

"Ana—" Cap's stern voice starts.

"You must be Ana Rocha." The FBI agent smoothly cuts off Captain Scott before taking a step toward me and offering a handshake. His voice isn't like before. It's done a 180. This must be something they teach in FBI school. I take his hand, hesitantly though. He has a firm grip and a charming smile. "Ben Smith. FBI."

"I figured as much."

His demeanor radiates with charisma. It would be impossible to tell that he was in a yelling match a few minutes ago. I wonder if all FBI agents come like this. "You must be Ana Rocha. Heard a lot about you when you caught the Attorney General's attention." He pauses. "You look tired, officer."

"Nothing I haven't dealt with."

He slightly nods. "I was hoping to run into you one of these days. Everyone says you're a damn good cop."

Cap's eyes go from Ben to me and then back to Ben, but he doesn't say anything. This is weird. The whole situation feels awkward. Why haven't they thrown me out yet for interrupting them? I had my rebuttal ready and everything.

Ben continues. "Your captain seems to be a bit overprotective of you. I was hoping to have had you as a part of the operation yesterday."

"He has his reasons."

"I'm sure." Ben glances back at Cap for a few long moments before his eyes gaze refocuses on me. "But all the same, you intruded at a perfect time."

It sure didn't sound like the perfect time.

"I'm sure you heard about yesterday's debacle," Ben continues.

"The whole world did." I take a deep breath. "And that's why I'm here."

Ben raises an eyebrow. "Really?"

I try to close the office door, but Ben's words stop me.

"Please. Leave it open, Ana."

It's an odd thing to ask, but I do what he says as I reply, "We're going to bring Ebony down and I'm going to spearhead it."

"…how?"

"If I get a confession, can you get her to sing?"

Ben slightly smiles. "I'll get her to dance."

"Officer Mend—" Cap starts.

Holding up his hand, Ben cuts Cap off. "Do you have a plan?"

"Not yet."

"Good. Because I have one."

"…what?" Is he serious? And if he is, why isn't he asking me to close the door? Shouldn't we be discussing this in private?

"I wanted to speak to you. There's a way we can still bring her down. But like I said, your captain seems to be a bit overprotective of you." Ben pauses. "Are you doing this for your sister?"

"So you know?"

"Word got out pretty quickly. Apparently, even Thorne knows about it. That's why I think she has someone in this station."

"Good."

"Ana." Cap comes out from behind his desk, "I won't allow you to do any such thing. What Ben is going to ask you to do is dangerous. Too dangerous for anyone."

"I have to, sir."

"No, you don't."

"It's the only way."

"Don't force my hand, Ana."

Ben looks over at him. "Scott, let—"

"I've heard enough from you!" Cap's fist slams onto his desk, silencing Ben. His gaze comes to me before he takes a deep breath. "You are leaving me with no choice here, Ana. I'm relieving you from duty by temporarily suspending you. You will give me your gun and badge. And then you will leave."

***

A few minutes later, Ben and I exit the office together. He lightly closes the door behind us. My heart is racing after everything that occurred inside. A part of me can't believe all this. But it's happening. With Cap's office door open, the entire station likely heard the commotion, which means that Ebony Thorne will soon know that I've lost my badge.

But that's what I'm counting on.

"…I'm sorry about what happened inside, Off—Ana."

I keep my eyes focused straight ahead, not glancing Ben's way. "It's not your fault. It's what had to happen."

"He was probably right though. You should rest."

"No time for that now." I start to walk away from him.

"…what are you going to do?"

"One of two things: die or…" I slightly turn my head back to look at him. "Shake this city up."

CHAPTER 16
DEN OF WOLVES

Bryan meets me at the appointed spot. My car doors are unlocked, and he takes a seat in the front passenger seat. He doesn't say anything immediately, keeping his gaze focused straight ahead. After a few long moments of silence, he finally looks my way. No doubt, he's second-guessing what he's come here to do. I don't blame him. I think a part of me is too. But today, I won't listen to that voice.

"You don't have to do this, Bryan. I've gotten you into enough trouble already."

"I think it's too late for turning back now, Ana."

"What did he say?"

"Hector said she'll be at *Desire* tonight. She'll be in the second-floor room with an out-of-state drug lord—Chung—who's negotiating a deal with her."

"Is he a big fish?" I ask.

"Not half as big as her. They'll be half a dozen armed hostiles in the place plus the bouncers."

I slowly nod. "Do you think she knows?"

"About your dismissal? Well, she has ears everywhere."

"Hopefully not in this car. Otherwise, we're all screwed."

Bryan slightly smirks.

I take a deep breath, thinking of what the night will hold.

"Ana… whatever you do…"

"Yes?"

I know what he's thinking. He's afraid. Afraid that he is sending another partner out to die. He shakes his head lightly, not saying the words that were about to escape his mouth. "Nothing, Ana. See you tomorrow, bright and early."

"As always, Bryan... as always."

***

I've never been to a nightclub before. The closest I've come is seeing them in the movies, and even those were far and few between.

I park a few blocks away and make my way there on foot. The streets are crowded with the type of people you'd expect to see in this part of town on a Friday night. This is not the type of place that I ever thought I'd be in.

But I ignore them all. Dressed in a pair of blue jeans and wearing a leather jacket over my shirt, I stick out from the crowds of lewdly dressed men and women. I see the building in the distance. The fluorescent lights reading "Desire" are a bright crimson. The club stands out from the other buildings. It seems to tower above them and almost possesses an intimidating presence.

My resolve grows stronger with every step. The closer I arrive, the more I think about one thing: Angela. I remember the endless rain splashing against me during her funeral. I remember my face being covered in tears and uncontrollably sobbing as I watched her body lowered into the grave. I remember how my heart screamed that day and every day since. I can still hear my mind refusing to accept the reality.

It's all brought me to this point.

Even from outside the walls, I easily hear the blaring music. There's a long line to get in. A bouncer at the door turns most people away. But tonight, I'm skipping the line. Without any hesitation, I walk past the crowd of indecently dressed patrons and straight toward the large bouncer. He sees me coming but doesn't seem alarmed. After all, I'm just a woman.

He puts his hand up. "There's a line, missy."

"My name is Officer Rocha." I maintain my stoic expression. "I have a warrant to search the premise."

There's an awkward pause. The whole crowd's focus is on me now. After what seems like a long moment, he suddenly sneers. "I was told about you. We all were. They said you might be coming tonight. But we all know you're not an officer. Not anymore."

"So you won't comply?"

"What I'll do is give you ten seconds to walk away before I shoot—"

Thump!

Before he gets a chance to finish his statement, he's picking himself up off the floor. I hear a gasp escape the onlookers as I knock him down with one quick strike to his guts and a second vicious blow to his head. But I don't give the bouncer a chance to recover. With a swift and powerful kick to the skull, he's out cold.

I turn around to face the line of clubbers. Their gazes travel from the unconscious bouncer and back to me in utter disbelief. This was definitely not what they were expecting tonight.

"Party's over, folks."

***

Inside the club, the dance floor is congested. The music is so brash that I'm half surprised the windows don't blow out. It seems that anybody would go deaf within ten minutes of it. But I don't pay it any more attention than it deserves. It's dark in here and I almost have to squint just to make out the silhouettes of everyone. The only lighting are LED club lights that continuously rotate. On the sides of the overcrowded dance floor are multiple bars.

Coming into the club, I immediately look toward my right. There's a spiral staircase leading to the second floor. At the top of the steps is a closed door. There is one man halfway up the staircase and two more sentries outside of the door. They're likely armed. But I don't care.

179

I take a deep breath. My eyes hold no fear. This job taught me that fear keeps you alive, but right now my soul is making me forget it. There are times when a person needs to use their brain. But I've learned that there are also times when you just need to beat the crap out of somebody. Right now is one of those instances.

I'm not afraid to die. Not tonight.

Let's do this, Ana.

Without any hesitation, I step toward the staircase. The men see me headed their way. They hesitate at first, thinking that I'm just a lost clubber. But the look in my eyes tells them what I'm here for. As I reach the foot of the stairwell, I see the closest man unsheathe a switchblade.

Don't hesitate, Ana. Not now.

"I'm an officer." I reach into my pocket where my badge and warrant would be. "I have a warrant to search upstairs."

He takes a step toward me, twirling his knife in an effort to intimidate me.

"I'm obligated to advise you that trying to stop me will be breaking the law. And I have the authority to use force." I take a deep breath. "But a part of me really wants to kick all of your asses."

The thug lunges at me.

Don't let him get close with that knife.

I sidestep his blade. I bring down my elbow onto his forearm, crashing his wrist into the stairwell's guardrail. He instinctively drops the blade and sends his other fist at me. I duck my head, avoiding it, before cross-facing him with my elbow. As he spits out blood and becomes momentarily stunned, I grab his head and violently slam it against the railing, knocking him out cold.

Perfect.

My heart's racing now. Sweat streaks down my cheeks. Vision is tunneled. But I don't care.

Nobody except the thug's comrades noticed the commotion. I look back toward the closed door. The two men see the fire in my eyes. I see the shock in theirs. If they were alone, they may have hesitated. And if they knew that I'm the one who killed Vinny the Rat, they may have even surrendered without a fight. But they think their numbers give them an advantage. People like them always travel in packs. That's the way it was when Angela was killed.

They're both stronger than me and have the high ground. But if I meet them near the top of the staircase, I'll have one major advantage against them.

I walk up toward them, fists clenched and eyes focused. We finally meet three-quarters up the staircase. No one hesitates.

Don't send in the first strike. Remember everything you learned in taekwondo. Let them make the first move—let them leave themselves exposed—then counter in the opening. Use the environment. The big one is the leader. He'll come at you first.

I duck, avoiding the big man's haymaker. The follower sends a blow, but I sidestep it. His other hand is holding a half-empty bottle of liquor. He sends it down at me, but I knock his hand away and force him to loudly break the bottle against the railing, spilling its contents all over the steps.

No wrong moves here, Ana. One blow and you'll fall down the stairs.

I don't think. I just react. I dodge the next strike from the leader. Stepping up, I grab his wrist before moving my foot to swipe his feet from behind. He tries to catch his footing, but it slips on the spilled alcohol. Before he realizes what's happening, he's violently tumbling down the steps.

The last goon lunges at me, fists swinging. He's faster than the other one. I weave my head to dodge the first strike. Then I evade the second. His fist passes inches away from my skull, but it leaves him a bit off-balance.

Now it's my turn to strike. Lowering my shoulder, I charge right into his guts. I hear him let out a groan as he loses his balance. He reaches for the railing, trying to regain his balance, but his fingers fall inches short. He follows his comrade down to the bottom of the steps. By the time he stops moving, he's out cold.

181

Keep moving, Ana.

I don't know if the commotion catches any notice. But I imagine that everyone down below is too preoccupied to notice.

Coming to the door, I open it with one great heave. It loudly swings on its hinges, revealing a corridor. At the end of the corridor is a single door which undoubtedly leads to the meeting room. But between me and the door is one heavyset man.

Before he has the chance to say a word or react, I reach behind me and whip out a pistol. He instinctively raises his hands with wide eyes. Looking between my face and my gun's barrel, he knows what happened to his friends outside.

"On your knees."

He slowly obeys as I move closer to him. The man tries to hide his fear in his voice. "You know how to use that thing?"

"Heard about Vinny the Rat?" Keeping my gun steadied on him, I move behind him. No false moves here, Ana. "Take a guess on who wasted him."

The guard doesn't say a word, but he gets the message.

You got one shot at this, Ana. Make it count.

Raising my pistol, I bring it down on the back of his head. The collision sounds off a loud echo and he immediately collapses. I take a moment to make sure he's not faking it. With a deep breath, I turn and look at the door.

Behind it is the culmination of everything. Angela's face burns brightly in my mind and so does the memory of her funeral. I don't know what will be behind this door. It may be my death. It may be closure. Or it may be proof that no matter how long I live, there is nothing I can do to ever regain the peace I lost.

But whatever it is, I'll embrace it with open arms.

***

Take a deep breath, Ana. The adrenaline is pumping through your blood. Use it to your advantage, but don't let it cloud your mind. Focus, Ana. Focus.

To be so close after all these years, with nothing more than a door separating me from the climax of all my pain—it feels surreal. But this is really happening. This is it.

Gun in hand, I quickly check to make sure that using it as a club didn't jam it. Seeing that it's still good to go, I slide the clip back in before looking back at the door. I shut my eyes, inhaling one more breath. One way or another, everything will end tonight. This is it.

My eyes open. Cocking back my leg, I send it down onto the door. The blow causes the very walls to tremor. The handle breaks and it swings wide open.

I go in, weapon raised.

There she is! Sitting at the end of a table is Ebony Thorne. My vision tunnels onto her. The world stops. For a moment, I think I'm dreaming. Our gazes lock. But when she sees me standing there with a gun, her eyes suddenly change—a hint of fear enters them. And when it happens, my mind returns to the reality of it all.

Behind her is her large bodyguard, Pedro. Chung sits opposite of her; his own bodyguard is armed with an AK47. But as soon as I charge into the room, all eyes are on me.

"Everybody freeze!"

My words fall on deaf ears. And in the next instant, all hell breaks loose.

Chung's bodyguard immediately aims his automatic rifle. But before he can fire a shot, I point my pistol at him and pull the trigger. My bullet violently rips through his shooting arm's shoulder, knocking him off of his feet. As he collapses, his head bangs against the hard table's side.

Pedro whips out his handgun and starts firing before I can pop off another shot. I instinctively fall to the ground. The roar of gunfire consumes the room, nearly shaking the walls. His first two bullets barely miss me. I feel them pass right over my head. By the time the third is shot off, I am running for cover and see Chung pick up his fallen lackey's AK47.

Taking refuge behind a thick and wide stack of drugs, I hear a few more of Pedro's bullets bury themselves into my barricade. His gun falls silent and I hear him reload, but then even louder gunfire engulfs the room as Chung pulls his rifle's trigger. The bullets violently crash against my defense, but none of them break through.

The gunfire is rancorous, each round more deafening than the last. My eardrums tremor. My skull is pounding. Chung's curses roar high above his weapon. One mistake, one stray bullet, and it's over.

Holding my gun with both hands, I take a deep breath. And then another.

Stay calm, Ana. Don't let the adrenaline get the better of you.

From this position, the only way they can get a clear shot is by flanking me or by climbing over my barricade. If they have any sense, they'll try the former. My back stays against the thick crate. The open door is only a few feet in front of me and to the right. I have to wait for the opportune moment to strike. I can't believe my heart rate is actually this calm.

I lightly close my eyes. The priority is Chung. He's the one with the AK. His gun falls silent with a click. I wait to hear him reload… but he doesn't. I didn't see him pick up any extra clips off his lackey. And if I can keep him from getting any, I will have the advantage. I don't need to hit him. Just scare him.

Without making myself visible, I aim my gun around the corner and blindly pull the trigger, hoping to nail Chung. I immediately hear him running. After three quick shots, I look out from behind my barrier and find that he's taken cover behind an overturned table.

Ebony is no longer where she was and Pedro is nowhere to be seen either. This is a stand-off. Holding my position, I keep my pistol steady. My gaze remains focused on Chung's barricade. I pull the trigger a couple of more times to ensure that Chung stays put. The bullets harmlessly bury themselves into his thick shield, but he gets the message.

Keep him trapped and I've got a shot at this.

Feeling something come from behind me, I twirl around as a new goon charges at me with a metal baseball bat in hand. I instinctively duck, dodging a swipe from his weapon. The bat violently smashes against the stack of drugs. I spring back up, trying to aim at him from point-blank range. But his bat crashes into my hand.

"Yah!" The yelp escapes me as my hand goes numb for a moment. My pistol hits the floor. And in the next instant, the thug kicks it away as pain engulfs my expression.

C'mon, Ana.

I scarcely dodge the next swing, feeling it pass right over my head. He tries to spear the top of his bat into my face, but I sidestep it. He may have experience in brawling, but he doesn't have the tact. Just by watching his eyes and hips, I can see what his next move will be.

Take away his advantage and then use it against him.

I take a half-step back as he takes a full step forward and sends another swing. I see it coming. I sidestep the blow and close the gap between us. Coming up to him, I grab the handle of his bat with one hand before my opposite elbow crashes into his face. Taking advantage of his dazedness, a swift kick to his guts forces him to let go of the weapon.

You're mine.

With a roar, I bring the bat down on his head. The collision sends a jolt up my own arms. There's a loud crack before he slumps to the floor. Instinctively, I twirl around and find Chung charging me. He brings his empty rifle down at me, but I sidestep it and crouch down as I step into him.

Holding the bat in the middle, I crash the handle into his stomach. I follow through by viciously jabbing the top of the bat against his chest. He stumbles backward. I've knocked the wind out of him. I need to take him out before Pedro shows up. I cock the bat back and let out a roar. Smashing the bat against his skull, Chung collapses onto the ground like my last victim.

I know he's coming. Without hesitating, I round the corner to take cover behind a stack of crates as Pedro arrives into view, pistol raised. His weapon roars as it discharges three bullets in quick succession, but he's a split second too late. Instead of nailing me, the bullets only hit air.

I don't have my gun. Crap. Rule number one: don't ever lose your gun. Bryan will kill me for this if Pedro doesn't.

Pedro is smart enough not to follow me around the corner, knowing that I'm waiting for him with a metal bat. As long as he has the gun, Pedro knows that he maintains the advantage. He'll keep his distance and wait me out. My hand that was struck by the bat is roaring with pain, but it's not broken. Adrenaline drowns out the pounding in my skull and most of my ache.

"You must be Ana." Pedro's voice sounds just like Vinny's: merciless and cold. "I've heard about you. I thought we'd come face-to-face at some point. Did you come here to die—to join your sister in the afterlife? Because that's the only way this ends."

I hear his heavy footsteps grow louder.

Pedro's malicious smirk is heard in his words. "And do you want to know the truth? Even after all you've done, after I kill you, nobody will still be able to touch us. Just like they could never touch us for anything else." He pauses. "Even your sister's death."

All reason washes away. It's replaced with something else: rage.

Doing a frontal role, I spring out from my cover and into his sight. Two bullets bounce on either side of me. He underestimates how quick my size makes me. With a mighty growl, I chunk my bat right at his face.

Pedro ducks, easily dodging it. But when he looks back up, I'm on him. With three strikes in quick succession, I make him drop his gun. I try to snatch the weapon up, but he delivers a strong kick, sending me sprawling onto my back.

I leap back onto my feet. His gun is in his hands. But his grin quickly disappears when he feels the weight of the pistol. The clip has been taken out, making the gun useless.

Pedro's voice does not lose any of its cruelty. "You have some quick hands, Ana."

He carelessly tosses the pistol aside. As he does, I finally notice the brass knuckles he's wearing on either hand. Pedro follows my gaze before looking back at me with a sinister smile. He intends to make an example out of me. He's going to show everyone what happens when someone tries to cross him and Queen Bee.

Too bad he chose the wrong gal.

He's big. But his size makes him slow. He'll want to fight in close quarters—try to get me in a corner where I have no choice but to take his blows.

Pedro comes at me. He sends three swift haymakers, each one of them strong enough to take my head off. But I keep my eyes focused on him. I duck to avoid the first blow before quickly sidestepping the next two as I slowly back up. He's more tactful than the goon who had the bat. He doesn't give any hints away by his movements. Pedro lets loose a couple of more quick blows. One of them gets dangerously close—close enough for me to feel the cold metal on his knuckles—but they all only hit air. He keeps going for headshots, knowing that even just one half-direct blow from him will knock me off balance.

He's relying on his brute strength. No finesse in him. Wait for your opportunity. One wrong move and he'll have you on the ropes. Don't let yourself get put in a corner.

Pedro's fist comes down again. Sidestepping it, I close the distance between us and cross-face him with my fist. My hand feels the impact of the blow, but I don't slow down. I follow through with my elbow and then my fist again. His jaw his tough. He doesn't spit out any blood but gets a good cut to the side of his mouth. But with each strike, I hear him lowly grunt with pain as he takes a step back.

He recovers quickly—quicker than I expected. Viciously deflecting my elbow, his free hand grabs me by my collar. He steps up and powerfully head bunts me square in the forehead. I hold back my cry of pain, but it floods me. Pedro violently shoves me into some heavy crates, knocking me off my feet. I land on my stomach and try to rise onto all fours without missing a beat. But his boot slams into my side, sending me back down.

I let out a groan of pain, feeling a stream of blood running down my face. Another kick sends me rolling back into the stack. Ache rings through my body. One of my ribs feels cracked and another seems broken. But all the pain momentarily disappears when a third kick lands on my head, finally causing me to cry out in pain.

Everything goes black. For a long moment, I can't feel anything. I can't think of anything else, except for the fact that this is the end. It's too much. *He's* too much. Even with everything, I can't beat him and I can't take down Ebony.

But then a face—a beautiful face—flashes before my eyes: Angela.

No. He's got me in the corner. But I'm not out yet. Not when I've come this far.

His boot comes down again, but I pull my head away at the last second. Doing a backward roll, I end up on my feet and sidestep his brass knuckles. I ignore the blood running down my face—I ignore everything. With a roar, my knee plunges into his stomach.

It doesn't slow him down. Pedro's fist aims for my head. I dodge it and grab his arm. I give it a quick twist as my foot nails him right between his legs. He lets out a loud groan and bends over in pain. Grabbing his head with both hands, I slam it into the wall. A thunderous bang sounds off with the collision.

Thud!

I do it again.

Bang!

And then again.

Crack!

Pedro is down for the count.

Looking at the unconscious body, I take a breath. Then another. *No time to waste, Ana.*

Moments later, I have my pistol back in hand. My hands are slightly trembling, but I try to block it out. There's still one thing left to do.

"Are you here to kill me?" Ebony's voice originates from the other side of a room. She's hiding behind a large filing cabinet. She must know that she's alone now. Her hired help has all but failed her. But her tone is different from before. It's not like it was at the Green Beetle Club. It's no longer in control. She's been so used to ordering violence from afar that she doesn't remember how to act when it happens right in front of her. Ironic.

I don't answer. I cock my weapon and slip off my shoes. She's out of her mind right now and is mine for the taking. If she was in control of herself, she would have attacked me when Pedro had me on the ropes. She would have at least shot at me. Instead, she was and is still hiding, too afraid to do anything.

"But I'll kill you first!"

Her hysteric words don't have enough confidence to intimidate a mouse. In fact, they hold more fear than conviction. Soundlessly, I make my way around the room—the long way.

"You're dead! Do you hear me! Nobody crosses me and lives!"

She's gone mad. Her voice is trembling, quivering with each and every syllable.

Ebony comes into view as I round the corner. Her back is turned toward me. Hiding behind a filing cabinet, she's quivering with fear as she clenches a handgun. After all this, is the fiend I've been after nothing more than a coward? Is she nothing more than a frail-hearted woman masked by her power and her strength?

I move in a little closer. She still doesn't see me. I'm almost on top of her now. I take aim from only ten feet away. I cock my weapon, slow enough that she hears every detail and knows that I have her.

"Drop it or die, Ebony."

Her gun loudly falls to the floor. Slowly, she turns to me, shivering more than ever. I finally see her eyes. They're no longer masked like they were in the club. They're no longer deceiving. Now, I see her true soul.

And Queen Bee—Ebony Thorne—is a coward.

Her fear-filled gaze is glued to my gun. She's covered in a cold sweat. "Ple—please do—don't kill m—me..."

My hands tighten around my weapon. Looking at her terror-stricken face, I see flashes of my memories: Angela's death, my parents' cries, the funeral, the loneliness, and my unanswered tears. She's responsible for it all. This coward is responsible for so much suffering in this city. And she did it without any remorse. "I came for only one reason, Ebony."

She collapses to her knees, arms raised above her head. "D—don't! What do you want me to say? I'll confess to it all!"

Ebony thinks I'll let this go? After everything she's done to this city and my family, she thinks I'll let *her* go? The thought makes the rage in my eyes go wild. My gun begins to slightly shake, but it's not from fear.

She sees it and starts to tremble even more. Tears run down her face as she sobs. "Do you want me to tell you that I'm the head of *Los Familia?* Do—do you want me to tell you that I'm the one who ordered the shooting that killed your sister? Do you want me to tell you that I'm the one responsible for half the drugs on the streets? Because it's all true! Every last word. I'll give you the names of everyone! Please don't kill me!"

"You think you deserve mercy!" My roar shakes the walls.

I feel my finger lightly push the trigger, but not hard enough to release a shot. I'm looking at the face of this city's most coldhearted criminal and she's begging me for mercy? She doesn't deserve mercy. She's never given mercy. Finger on the trigger, every impulse screams for me to pull it. To end her. To kill this monster.

...but I don't. A voice suddenly rings in my head—Angela's voice. And with just one word, my sister washes away all the rage.

No, Ana. She deserves to die, but you don't deserve the blood on your hands.

For a long moment, I feel as if Angela is standing next to me. It's as if she's telling me to do the thing my heart and mind refuse to do.

But I listen to her.

Slowly, I lower the gun. Ebony looks at the lowered weapon and then back at me in disbelief. My opposite hand comes out from behind my back. In it is a tape recorder. I take a deep breath. "I'm not going to kill you, Ebony. I came to put an end to all this. I came to ensure that nobody else will ever be hurt because of you. As for your death... I'll let the courts decide that. But before they do, they'll use every ounce of knowledge in your brain to take down everything you've built."

As I say those words, I hear a commotion downstairs. The music abruptly stops. It's replaced by chaos as a sea of uniformed officers flood the building. I holster my weapon and pull something else from my pocket: my badge. And I follow it by throwing a piece of paper at Ebony's feet. One look at it tells her what it is: a warrant. A federal warrant.

"Ebony Thorne, you're under arrest."

CHAPTER 17
PEACE

It doesn't take long for my backup to reach me. Ebony is whimpering like a dog when the handcuffs are put on. She is taken away by several FBI agents along with the rest of the unconscious goons. When the police and agents see her in this state, they can hardly believe that they're looking at the most dangerous criminal in Houston.

I'm soon whisked away. The rest of the night is one mixed blur. But the one thing I do know for certain is that Bryan stays with me the entire time. He is there when they stitch me up and patch up my wounds. He's there when I'm debriefed. And he's there when everything is explained to the rest of the police force.

Half of them can't believe it when they're told that my dismissal was just a ruse. We were betting on Ebony having a mole at the station who would tell her of my discharge. If Ebony had known that I was a cop, she would have known that I wouldn't pull the trigger. But thinking I was just a vigilante with nothing to lose, she was willing to say anything to save her life, even confess to her crimes. After the recent disaster, no local judge would give a warrant, but Ben was able to pull some strings and get a federal judge to issue one.

A good part of the late night is spent in my office. I collapse on the chair, too exhausted to do anything else. The adrenaline of it all has finally worn off. My mind and energy level plummets as reality sets in. I just want to sleep, but I don't get the chance. Person after person comes in to congratulate me on a job well done, but I don't know if I answer them back or not. I don't even recognize most of them. Half of them are dressed like federal agents.

"Well done, Ana."

"That took some guts."

"Proud of you."

The words seem to go in one ear and out the other. My mind's so full that it can't compute anything right now. I honestly just want to be left alone.

The entire time, I can't believe it's done. After all these years, it's all finally over. It feels like a part of me ended with my quest. I don't know if what I did will give Angela peace. Now that it's all done and the quest is over, I don't think any of it ever mattered to her. Her soul was at peace the moment her life ended. But what I do finally possess for the first time in years is something I've sought after for a long time:

Clarity.

***

It's only half an hour until dawn when I finally arrive home. I don't sleep. My eyes and body want to shut down, but rest is the last thing my mind is thinking of. Within a couple of hours, Bryan shows up at my front door. From the look of it, he hasn't slept either. He cooks me breakfast. We don't say much. We're both exhausted, but neither of us is considering sleep after last night.

Bryan can certainly whip up a mean scrambled egg. And after he adds a couple of warm slices of toasted bread covered in melted butter, it's a meal to remember. But I'm unable to bring myself to compliment him and we end up eating in silence. I wouldn't even know what to say if I could talk.

Soon after breakfast is finished, I finally begin to feel sleep overtake me as I sit on the end of my living room's couch. But a loud knock on the door wakes me back up. Bryan opens it and finds Cap and Ben on the other side. Their eyes are just as red as ours. Seems like nobody at all got any sleep.

For as long as I've known Cap, he's always been a cleanly shaven man. But his face is covered in a stubble today morning.

Shortly after joining us in the living room, Cap breaks the silence. "How are you feeling?"

"…tired, but restless."

He slightly smiles. "You're probably just hungover on the nerves of it all. Every soldier goes through it."

"Yeah… probably."

"Thank God you got out of it all okay."

There's a moment of awkward silence before Ben speaks. "What you did last night is all the news is reporting. You've even got the entire FBI talking. Of course, we'll keep your name under wraps from the press."

There's a brief silence.

"Ana…" Ben pauses. "I've been doing this for a long time. But you are the most foolhardy and bravest cop or agent that I've ever seen. I don't know of another person who would have charged into the lion's den like you. And to come out in one piece is something else."

I nod in appreciation. I guess that's his way of saying 'thank you'.

"Rest assured, we've got Ebony," Ben continues. "That confession ties everything else together. She'll get life in prison. No matter how much information she's willing to dish out, we won't let her get off. As we speak, we're having agents and officers pick up her lieutenants. They already have an angle on her. Queen Bee—along with her organization—is history."

"I hope you can follow through on the promise," I reply. "She's hurt a lot of good people."

"We will."

Cap looks over at me. "You can take as long as you need, Ana. But whenever you're ready, you'll have a lot of options. A lot of people have heard about what you did. The governor himself wants to talk to you, and I bet it'll be more than just a simple congratulations."

"I've spoken to my superiors about you," Ben adds. "And they say there is a place in the FBI for you if you want it.."

I slightly nod without saying anything.

They stay for a little while longer. They talk, but it's more among themselves and with Bryan. They can see that I'm not all there and respect that enough. I hear Bryan promise them to stay by my side for today. After a few minutes, they finally depart.

My partner and I sit there for a long time without saying a word. The only sound is the ticking of the clock behind us. Bryan waits patiently as last night's events replay in my head over and over again. I see it all: the faces, the onslaught, Ebony's fear. It happened only a few hours ago, but it already feels like a distant dream.

"It's over…" I whisper. "It's all finally…over."

Bryan is slow to respond. "You did it, Ana. Your sister can rest in peace now."

Slowly, I look away from the floor and at him. "I don't think the dead care about vengeance. Neither Angela nor Jack." I pause. "Maybe we've just been doing this to ourselves."

"Maybe…" He thinks for a moment. "When all the ceremonies are done, do you know what you want now?"

"No…"

"You don't need to do this anymore. You finished what you set out to do."

"I did… didn't I? And through it all, you were at my side, Bryan. I would have never made it far without you. You were always there… thank you."

He smiles without saying a word.

I take a deep breath. "With Ebony gone, I don't know if I have the drive for this anymore. I did it all for Angela. But I don't know what to do next." There's a brief silence. "But before I do anything else, there's something we both have to take care of."

***

For the first time, I show Bryan the room that has been dedicated to Angela's death. He sees the web of facts that surround my beautiful sister's face. He sees the countless questions that are taped to the wall and all the arrows that crisscross one another. He now understands what has been driving me for all this time.

It has served its purpose. For the past months, it constantly reminded me why I was doing all this. It kept the motivation in front of me every day. But now, we both know what we need to do. It's the only thing left to do before I can fully move on with my life. We don't say anything—there's nothing that needs to be said. He knows why I'm showing this to him.

We take it down together. I don't cry. I don't hesitate. I don't even second-guess myself. It's time. With every action, I sense Angela's smile. It seems to grow stronger with each thing that is stripped from the wall. It happens so fast. Soon, there is nothing there except for her picture. But I know that it has to go too. Angela has been at peace since she left this world. Now, it's time that I let go. It's time that I have my peace.

This alone won't do it. But it'll be a good start. Good enough.

***

When mama opens the front door, she can hardly believe that it's me standing there. She lets out a quick gasp and covers her mouth. I had an entire speech prepared to tell her how sorry I was. To tell her what a fool I was for pushing her away and to tell her that I would never do it again. But when I see her eyes and her glowing face, I can't say a word. Instead, my eyes say it all.

A smile suddenly spreads across her face. It's bigger and more joyous than any I've ever seen. It's followed by tears streaming down her face. The light is back in my life. I'm suddenly in her arms.

And for the first time in years, our family feels whole again.

***

From afar, I watch as Bryan and Mary sit on a park bench. It's been months since they've seen each other, but the fact that she agreed to meet him here says something. Actually, it says almost everything. And the fact that they're holding hands only amplifies it.

The park is nearly empty on this weekday morning. The skies are clear and a beautiful sun shines down on the couple. It all seems too perfect. There are even birds chirping. Or maybe that's just my mind playing tricks on me.

I can't help but smile. I've seen Bryan go from the tough, no-nonsense cop to a friend. And now, we've both changed each other's lives for the better. On this journey to make myself feel whole again, I never thought about what my actions might do. But it now turns out that maybe I've played a small part in helping another family reunite as well.

And that alone makes it all worth it.

***

It's been a couple of weeks since Ebony went down. She's been more than willing to tell the FBI everything she knows. Apparently, her elderly father could be implicated in a couple of her crimes. But for her testifying, the FBI will leave him out of this and let him live out the rest of his cancer-sickened life in a retirement home.

Ebony will be receiving the death penalty, even after confessing to everything. But she'll have a lot of her friends with her on Death Row. It'll be a nice final reunion for the lot of them.

I've been invited to the governor's office next week. I received a letter from him—handwritten—congratulating me. But he wants to meet me in person to give me an award and talk about a new job. I even received a letter from Ben's boss. Ben has been promoting me to his colleagues and department, making his superior keen on speaking with me. However, I'm not even sure if I want to do anything with law enforcement anymore though.

Bryan and Mary have started seeing a counselor now. They even moved back in with one another. Both of them realized how much they need each other and are trying to make it work. I think they will. Kevin was ecstatic when he saw his dad finally return home. This time, they'll be starting everything on the right foot. They both know what's most important.

My brother and sister-in-law have started making preparations for their upcoming arrival. It'll be a baby girl. They already have a name picked out. It's a name that only an angel could ever have. There'll be a baby shower in a couple of weeks, and I would not miss it for the world.

I haven't been to work since the shakedown, but I've met up with Bryan and Mary several times. The man seems like an entirely new person. He spends more time smiling—genuinely smiling—than not and you can feel the love they have for each other. They are going on a fishing trip next weekend and asked me to come with them.

But I doubt that my mom will let me out of her sight for that long after getting me back. I think she knows now. Maybe not the specifics, but she understands that I've done what I had to do. She knows that I lied to her. She may not know the full truth, but I don't think she cares.

I've even started going back to church. My parents didn't force me. They were surprised to wake up one Sunday and find me getting ready to go. And when I did go, I didn't feel anything there but bliss. I've finally truly come home.

Ever since reuniting with my parents, I've been living with them. I sleep in Angela's old room—something I could never imagine doing even a few weeks ago. The room is just the same as it always was, down to the very wallpaper. Yellow was always her favorite color and it's growing on me now.

Normally, I sleep like a baby every night. But slumber stays far away tonight. It's not nightmares. I haven't had those in days now. It's just the knowledge that I'll soon need to decide what to do next. There are so many roads at my feet that I don't know which way to step. It's as if there is no perfect path for me anymore.

I don't know what brings me to do so, but when midnight rolls around, I find myself rummaging through Angela's old stuff. This isn't the first time I've looked through it. I don't know what I expect to find or what brought me to do his. Maybe it's just restlessness.

Going through a chest, I look past many of Angela's old toys: dolls, stuffed animals, play sets, and so much more. These were things that she had once intended to pass down to me. But I didn't dare touch them after she left us.

My hand grazes something unfamiliar. I grasp it with my fingers and pull it out. It's a letter. I've been through this chest a hundred times and have never seen it. And my heart nearly stops when I see who it's addressed to:

FOR MY BEAUTIFUL SISTER

Why have I never seen this before? Cautiously, I pull the note out of the envelope. It smells just like her. My hands are unconsciously shaking as they hold it. This can't be happening. I must be dreaming.

I unfold the letter and stare at the note. It's in her handwriting. The ink has faded, but the words remain clear. And within two sentences, tears are streaming down my face. My sobs consume the closet and my heart begins to race with a mix of joy, sorrow, and hope.

Ana,

My dear sister. You'll never know how much I love you. The more I help those less fortunate than me, the more my eyes are opened. I hear their stories and have seen things that I will never share with anyone else.

You're growing into a beautiful young woman. One day, you'll have the world in your hands. I know it. And when that day comes, you may come to learn what I have learned. You and I have lived in light, but there is much darkness and evil in the world. I've learned that you can't have both innocence and justice. I pray that you choose innocence. I pray that you choose to live your entire life in the light. It is by far the more convenient choice. But if you feel led, then choose the latter.

Choose to make the world a better place.

***

The sun is only halfway above the horizon when I stand at the foot of Angela's tombstone. I take a deep breath as I run my hand along the curved top. It feels like an eternity since I last stood here. Last time, I was so lost. I made the vow to do whatever it took to bring down criminals: lie, cheat, steal, and even kill. I've done all of those. I now realize how close I was to crossing a line on that day. It was a line that I would never have been able to come back from.

But now... now everything seems so clear.

"I'm sorry if I ever disappointed you, Angela." I take a deep breath. "It wasn't Ebony who tore me apart—she's not the one who plunged me onto the dark path... I did that myself. But... I now know what my guiding star is. It's always been there for me. I just needed to open my eyes to see it."

I smile.

"It's you. It's always been you." I pause for a moment. "And I've made my choice, Angela. I've seen the light and I've seen the darkness. I've walked the line between them. And now, I've made the choice. Not the choice that you prayed I would make... but the one that will make you proud. And the one I've been called to do."

ABOUT THE AUTHORS

AMMAR HABIB

Ammar Habib is an award-winning and bestselling author who was born in Lake Jackson, Texas in 1993. Ammar enjoys crafting stories that are not only entertaining, but will also stay with the reader for a long time. Ammar presently resides in his hometown with his family, all of whom are his biggest fans. He draws his inspiration from his family, imagination, and the world around him.

Other works by Ammar include:
The Heart of Aleppo
Memories of My Future
Dark Guardian
Dark Guardian: A New Dawn
Dark Guardian: Legends

To learn more about Ammar, please visit:
www.ammarahsenhabib.com

GLENDA MENDOZA

Glenda Mendoza has two decades of law enforcement experience serving in the Greater Houston Area. She has served in many capacities, including working as a Deputy Jailor, Patrol Officer, Narcotics Investigator, Special Investigative Unit Agent, involving various vice investigations and a District Attorney Investigator. Her experiences helped keep this novel authentic and ensured that Ana Rocha's character remained true to life. Glenda currently works as a Threat Management Detective, working mental health investigations and criminal investigations involving threats of danger.